THE LAND OF KEIKITRAN AND ELEEVAN

R. G. H. Siu

The Land of Keikitran and Eleevan
by R. G. H. Siu

Contact Information:
The International Society for Panetics
6186 Old Franconia Road
Alexandria, VA 22310

Published by Hats Off Books™
610 East Delano Street, Suite 104, Tucson, Arizona 85705, U.S.A.
www.hatsoffbooks.com

International Standard Book Number: 1-58736-075-6
Library of Congress Control Number: 2001119033

Printed in the United States of America

A LETTER OF TRANSMITTAL

Dear Dave:

At long last my travel report on that fascinating country of Chianglai and her gentle people has been put into reasonable shape. After getting you all excited about its unique approach to government, I must apologize for not getting it into your hands earlier—especially before your recent consulting swings through several African capitals.

I would have been completely lost with their strange rationale, had it not been for the good fortune of having known Chianglai's chief theoretician, Thak. We were very close friends decades ago, sharing an attic flat in Montparnasse and pooling our last francs on many an occasion for a bottle of *Beaujolais*. He not only accompanied me on some of the visits, patiently clarifying the subtle compatibility of seeming inconsistencies, but also arranged a sequential agenda, which revealed in a stepwise fashion how their basic theory of government unfolds naturally into practical impacts upon the lives of the people.

I believe the Laians might have developed one of the next evolutionary options to the socialist state, the Great Society, or whatever you may wish to designate the political tendency of the latter half of the twentieth century.

From what I was able to see during the three-week trip, the people there are quite happy. Their morals decorous. Their morale high. Their outlook confident. Their love for all things living—here I confess an ability to find an adjective that describes it precisely—touched me very, very deeply.

But enough of this chatter. Enclosed are the travel highlights. Please feel free to make use of the contents in your own work. I mentioned this possibility to

Thak. He has no objection. He did caution, however, against injudicious adoption of foreign ideologies and practices. I agree and I'm sure you do as well.

As ever,

G.H.
Washington, D. C.
May 12, 1972

Table of Contents

TRAVEL HIGHLIGHTS

The Capital

TERKUNG

1

"Welcome to Chianglai!"—a familiar voice cried out at the foot of the steps beside the plane. Sounded as if it came thirty six years ago from my skinny roommate in Montparnasse. Now it belongs to the National Administrator for Policy and Planning, the fourth ranking man in the country.[*]

Thak led me directly to his car. He handed my passport and baggage checks to the aide. "Your bags will be brought to our guest cottage, where you will be staying the next three days or so. It's certainly good to see you after all these years, G. H. I know you love wine, or used to anyway. I've collected samples of Chianglai's finest to celebrate your visit. Let's try some over at my place. By the way, have you ever gotten around to paying back our rent? Fine. Otherwise we ought to wire some money to our embassy in Paris right now to take care of that wonderful landlady, her son, grandson, or somebody. I'll never forget those days. And especially you—good old G. H.—you, who shared your last sou with me." At the house, I tried to tell him about the work I had planned for the three-week trip and my desire to make use of every minute of it. But he wouldn't listen. "Tomorrow morning, we can talk business. Tomorrow morning, maybe ten o'clock. Not tonight. Tonight is for friendship . . . for wine . . . for the spirit. More wine, G. H.?"

And so the evening went, just like the old days of poetry and philosophy, of nibbling sausages and sipping *Beaujolais* in an attic flat in Montparnasse.

Finally turned in at 4:10 A.M., Thursday.

---

[*] A description and history of Chianglai is presented in Appendix I.

2

Got up a little after nine. What a picturesque setting: Bedroom windows over-looking the bend of a small pond. Chaste flowers of the sacred lotus rising a foot above the placid surface, broken now and then by the splashing tail of the mullet. Two-horned frogs and little turtles afloat on the buoyant leaves. Pandanus, laced with morning glories with their profusion of pink funnels. Farther back, 100-foot teaks with their large oval leaves and candelabras of white blossoms. Not a human sound. Only the warbling of birds and the soughing of the breeze. And the whole place perfumed by the ginger and jasmine.

Washed quickly. As I entered the living room, the aide greeted me with a cheerful "*Bonjour!*" and announced that breakfast was being served. On the table were *Le Figaro*, which had just been delivered by the morning plane, and a note from Thak. He hoped that I slept comfortably, asked that I enjoy a leisurely break-fast, and advised that the aide will see me to his office at my convenience. I gulped down the ham and eggs and wasted no time getting there. After exchanging some pleasantries and inquiring over my well-being, Thak offered a tentative agenda and itinerary for my approval.[*]

Three days here at Terkung for talks with senior officials and intensive briefings on the philosophy of the good life and the government's approach toward its realization by the Laians. Weekend sightseeing around the Capital. Then two days at Prakung, visiting a Community. Three days at the Saikung Regional Headquarters, visiting universities, an industrial plant, criminal justice operations, and an art center. Weekend outing in the nearby Sonbang National Park. Two days at Maikung, visiting additional regional activities, namely, a research institute, Chianglai's largest agricultural complex, a metropolis manage-ment agency, and an ecology management agency. Two days at Pnomkung, visit-ing the military headquarters of the Eastern Sector. One day back at Terkung for final discussions and questions and answers. Overnight cruise down the Wakong River to Haikung. Then home.

All of my wishes and more had been anticipated. I could not think of any-thing to add.

---

[*] Itinerary is mapped out in Appendix II.

3

Thak took it upon himself to present the initial orientation. He placed considerable importance upon my acquiring an intuitive feel of the spirit of what he was going to say. What the theoretician regarded as empirically certain throughout history are: (1) Men are born unequal and different. Moron to genius. Ugly to handsome. Congenital detects to perfect health. Miserable surroundings to excellent. (2) No man is endowed in every single trait more favorably than all others. No man can assure himself that his own descendants will be as richly or as poorly endowed as he. No man is self-sufficient. The more fortunately blessed in a particular aspect are in a better position to, assist others than those less so. (3) Suffering is universal. Some deep-seated, such as anxiety and loneliness. Some self-generated, such as ambition and envy. Some accidental, such as contagious diseases and automobile collisions. Some caused by strangers, such as military invasions and internal robberies. Some by fellow citizens, such as inept management and corrupt bureaucracy. (4) Men vary in their source of happiness and the intensity of their quest for it. Some contented with little. Some seek it in grandsons. Some in art. Some in literature. Some in leisure. Some in material possessions. Some in prestige. Some in power. (5) Great power is exercised only through organized groups. Oppression occurs when members holding the reins of power end up excessively better off than other contributors to the social good without power, such that the latter are driven below the level of essential requirements of sheer living. Exploitation occurs when the latter is driven below the level of reasonable equity. Bewilderment occurs when different institutions issue binding directives backed up by compulsions of some kind to the same individual. Imperialism occurs when one of these parties is alien to the country. (6) All men desire a protector against the invader, the murderer, the robber, the raper, and the bully. (7) All men crave a feeling that someone cares for them, especially one who can support and/or protect them. (8) All men understand the good life as one that is good in its entirety—birth, youth, adult, old age, death. Satisfying relationships with family, friends, strangers. Belonging to something lasting, to which they are contributing. A sense of meaning in their lives. (9) All men value privacy and some personal things they can call their own, something they can treasure, somebody they can love. Most need some being they can worship. (10) An absolute limit exists in the natural resources of a country and a relative limit in the producible and replaceable wealth.

These ten empirical premises (there are more) underlie the plans, programs, and operations of Chianglai's system of social regulation. The national objectives of highest uncompromising priority are: defense against invasion, provision of essential biological needs for all citizens throughout their lives, and *de facto* power in the hands of the people. Second priority: security of the person against violence, pervasive feeling throughout the country of fairness and reasonableness and sense of identity and belonging among practically all citizens. Third priority: guaranteed employment for all in consonance with physical and mental capacities; appropriate rest and leisure for all; respect for everyone's personal privacy, worship, and family life; minimum of high school education for everyone. Fourth priority: assimilation of new ideas and values for the continuous enrichment of Laian culture, development of the full potential of the specially gifted in all phases of human endeavors. "Our system of government is based upon these historical lessons and Laian values," said Thak in conclusion. "How well we in the National Chamber of Deputies discharge our duties is determined solely by how well the goals are attained. Did not some German scientist say a hundred or so years ago that the most beautiful theory can be ruined by a single ugly fact? In like manner I would say that the good name of the national Chamber of Deputies and the National Administration can be ruined by a single unrelieved starving stomach or a single unattended sick man in Chianglai."

As we left the conference room, Thak turned to me for a favor. "With the candor of long friendship," he said, "at the end of your visit, good G. H., will you answer yes or no—without any further explanation, just yes or no—to each of the following two questions: First, do you feel that every one of the officials you met on the trip is striving to live up to the philosophy and aspirations just outlined? And second, do you feel Chianglai will achieve the objectives within our lifetimes?" I promised to do so. There was a kind of dedicated silence for a full five seconds, when Thak finally exclaimed: "Well, so much for business. Let's have some food. Incidentally, I forgot to tell you. The Senior National Administrator has invited us over to his home for dinner. Nothing fancy. Just the three of us. You'll like Administrator Nam."

4

What cuisine! Entree was *canard à l'orange*, but with the delicious golden brown crispy skin that I've savored only once years ago in a little restaurant in an alley in

Peking. Nam was a genial host, with a twinkle in his patient eyes, set in a kindly face rising from a determined jaw. He was open and candid as I tried to understand his preoccupations as the loader of his people.

What is the one thing that concerns him more than anything else? "Maintaining an unconquerable faith among the Laians, a stability of confidence, a sinking of deep anchorage into the very bowels of the country. The love of the land, the rivers, the mountains, the trees, the animals, the people—the places where their ancestors lived, the forests they tended, the hills they terraced, the channels they dredged, the fields they plowed—this is Chianglai. This is where the Laians come from. This is where they will return. This is they." Given this dedicated sense of belonging among the people, "no army on earth will be sufficiently powerful to subdue us." Given this dedicated sense of belonging among the officials, "no man, woman, child, beast, bird, or tree in Chianglai will be mistreated." Nam considers keeping such a national temper intensely alive to be his prime purpose for existence. To him, operating the governing apparatus itself is of secondary importance. "Much better an ill-administered bureau with genuine love for the people and Nature around us, than an efficient group of technicians with well balanced statistics and impressive charts."

What potential danger to his country does he dread most? "The supplanting of the instinctive attachment for the land and her people by an intellectual patriotism of the country as the stockroom of material possessions." So much of the latter philosophy is prevalent throughout the world that Chianglai is reluctant about enlarging its cultural contacts with the West beyond her capacity of assimilation without distortion of her essential values. "Otherwise within two generations, Chianglai can be reduced to a winter resort of Judeo-Christian materialism. I do not fear military invasions as much as I fear ideological ones. The former we can see and resist. But ideological invasions are much more insidious, especially the pitting of citizen against citizen for material advantage. We do not set brother against brother. We do not separate ourselves into competitor *we* and competitor *they*. We try to find a reasonable accommodating and sharing together. Such an atmosphere must prevail throughout the land as naturally as the oxygen we breathe, if life here is to be good spiritually as well as physically." On that note, we bid each other goodnight.

5

With the aid of many lucid charts[*] Naaouk, who is Chief of National Planning in Thak's Department, explained the government apparatus and philosophy. The country is divided into ten regions, each with a population three to five million. Each region consists of about two hundred communities, each with a population of about ten to fifty thousand. The National Chamber of Deputies is the highest governing body. It operates foreign affairs and plans and supervises all social activities in the country. Personal and intra-family matters are left to the individual residents. The Region Chambers of Deputies operate the national enterprises in accordance with the national plans and supervise the social programs of the communities. The Community Chambers of Deputies operate local activities.

Within the community, citizens above the age of sixteen vote for the hundred members of the Community Chamber for a term of six years. After two years in office, the Community Chamber elects from among its membership a new Chairman of the Chamber the nine new members of the Community Adjudication Panel, and one representative to the higher Regional Chamber. The new Chamber of the Community Chamber also assumes the position of Senior Community Administrator in charge of program execution. He appoints a Vice Senior Administrator, an Ombudsman, and four program administrators from the membership of the Chamber. The designees, in turn, appoint successors from their respective communities to fill out the unexpired terms in the Community Chamber. An analogous process takes place at the Regional and the National levels.

There appears to be no other way to social power than this monolithic structure. The public owns all of the major resources that can serve as a base for significant power. Land is only on loan from the people. Although certain individuals such as inventors, writers, artists, and calligraphers may accumulate considerable personal wealth, private property is limited to possessions directly tied to the efforts of the family. "Where is freedom for the individual in Chianglai?" I interrupted.

---

[*] The four principal organization charts are reproduced in Appendix III.

Naaouk tried very hard to be convincing in his statements about how freedom is guaranteed the individual in Chianglai. But it was no use. There was no real communication between us, sincere though he was in his attempt. To him, freedom is a derivative state of mind, flowing from the actual condition of life, rather than a postulated principle for which provisions are to be attempted toward its realization. Round and round the same track he went. Each time he would speak more slowly and pronounce his French words more distinctly, feeling that perhaps my obvious dissatisfaction with his explanations was due to his imperfect pronunciation. But we always ended up where we began.

"The greatest slavery is that of a conquered and oppressed people, with which we have had much painful experience. Would you agree?" I nodded. "Equal to that is starvation, illness, and deplorable biological deficiencies. Would you also agree?" I nodded again. "That is why we have placed freedom from these two fears number one in our national priority. Does this make sense?" I found myself nodding a third time. "Well, our country is poor. We are technologically behind. We have many uneducated people. It is so easy for a clever man to steal the tattered clothes off their backs and the few grains of rice from their bowls if the former were allowed the freedom to do as he pleases. There is no one who can effectively care for the ignorant, the poor, and the weak, except the more fortunate and the dedicated. That is why our government. . . ." By this time I gave up arguing and decided to sit it out. "Now, our people are kind by nature. They are reasonable. As a consequence they become very ill at ease whenever someone orders them to do such and such a thing *or else*. That is why we have panels of adjudication rather than courts of law. There is a greater flexibility of reasonableness in the negotiations among adjudicators than in the decisions of judges resting on the letter or technicalities of the law. Incidentally, we make no *Laws* in Chianglai; we propose *Citizens Prescriptions*. Again, there is an implied latitude for understanding deviations in the very name itself. And everybody understands it as such. Coming back to the subject of adjudication, before each hearing the counsels representing both sides formally attest to a genuine commitment to search for the truth as they see it without intentional distortion of any kind. The whole concept of adjudication being that after considering the various views of the facts and extenuating circumstances, the two sides and the adjudicator can arrive at a common acceptable disposition of the case. This approach to jurisprudence provides the citizens with a third freedom: the freedom from the cunning, the severe, and the arbitrary." "I don't think the American Bar Association would buy that at all!"—I amused myself with the thought. "Another thing, our brethren are very trusting in character and like to please others. They become terribly upset whenever they are placed under conflicting orders by two or more authorities. If we let this situation prevail as a normal condition of life, our people will gradually lose their Laian personality and will become dissembling, hard-hearted, and litigious. They will no longer be Laians; they will be some other breed. Our system protects the people from this dilemma by restricting the access to social power to the simple political mechanism controlled by the Laian people themselves. That is one reason why we rotate men in and out of positions of ruling authority by limiting them to a term and a half at any given echelon. That is why we allow no foreign institution to give orders to our brethren—be it in the form of economic, cultural, or religious means. Our people are free to think and believe whatever they please in their personal lives. But as to the issuance of a command affecting the social relationships among their brethren—no, that is not right. In this way, we assure the people's freedom from bewilderment." And so the session went on and on.

All this must have indeed appeared logical to Naaouk, because his eye beamed with earnest dedication as he spoke. It all struck me, however, as so much Marxist velvet over a totalitarian régime. But Naaouk and his staff were most considerate and courteous through what must have been a trying morning. For my own part I tried to reciprocate, although I admit that I must not have been as successful at it.

7

Recognizing that there was no further point in pursuing the basic rationale behind their trans-socialist framework, I tried to shift our attention in the afternoon session to those specific areas which may have application within any philosophy of government. Perhaps I might learn something of value there. The system of justice had been covered during the earlier period. The emphasis on culture had been explained very well by Nam at his home. That on national planning follows naturally from a trans-socialist state. I decided to begin with their unusual organizational alignment of military affairs.

Why did they combine foreign affairs and the armed forces under the National Administrator for Foreign Affairs? "That is the only way to unify our approach to the outside world. Military forces are but one of the instruments of international relations, which we hope will not be resorted to in our relationships with others. No, the Senior National Administrator is *not* the Commander-in-Chief of the Armed Forces. He does control them, of course, but only through the command line in the National Administration. The Senior National Administrator's primary role is that of insuring an integrated and balanced harmony of the total needs of the people as a whole. We do not feel that he should have a preferential personal operating responsibility over a few special activities. This can only tend to distort the national priorities, resulting from a subconscious emphasis on those particular segments. The arrangement whereby the head of state serves as direct Commander-in-Chief of the Armed Forces would, in my opinion, be most efficient for a militantly expanding empire. But our military strategy is one of a defensive character, as you will see when you visit Pnomkung." Is there a nationwide leader of any religious sect in Chianglai? How are the religious institutions supported? "Religion is considered to be a personal matter. There is no national religious leader who controls any of our fifty-six recognized sects in the country. Each community has its respected religious teachers. One of them becomes revered as the wisest and most virtuous of all. This person, in effect, then becomes the inspirational primate. He is neither elected, appointed, nor recognized as such. He has no authority to dictate beliefs to anyone, but only to teach and guide. But somehow the word gets around as to who such a man is and the communicants invariably recognize him almost unanimously. As a rule, such a leader gains the deep respect of the people outside of his own religion as well. The pastor controls no funds other than what he gets in donations from his own flock. Each head of a Laian household is provided a hundred lai-yuans per year (about three per cent of earnings) for religious or charitable purposes as he sees fit. The National Administration subsidizes half of the costs of needed church construction requested by the community religious leader." How successful have your ombudsmen been? "The service has proven to be one of the most valuable in our society. Only the wiser, more patient, and more compassionate men are appointed to these positions. Sometimes, men are asked to serve for a term between operating responsibilities. Sometimes, men retired from high government posts. The ombudsmen are authorized to write directly to any office in the country, which they feel capable of assisting the resident in distress. Their analyses of the problem and recommendations for alleviation are always given most careful consideration. If failures to render effective help are thought by them to be unresponsive, they would appeal to the Adjudication Panel for final disposition. Situations rarely reach such a state and the cases get quick attention whenever there are indications of such possibilities. For a government official to be invited by the Adjudicator to explain anything is regarded as a major disgrace in itself. Because of the ready accessibility of the ombudsmen and their evident sense of caring and ability to get action, no resident of Chianglai ever feels being pushed aside without being given a sympathetic attempt at his problem." What is that organizational block called "Personal Subsidies"? "That is a place where anyone can go for financial help on problems of a personal nature, which is not included in the standard social programs. There are not many circumstances requiring money, which are not so covered. But they do arise occasionally. And when they do, we do not want our brethren to feel that they have no place to which to go. For example, I read a report yesterday about a poor young man who lost his wallet on the way to the tourist office to pay for the bus tickets and hotel reservation for his three-day honeymoon next week. The Personal Subsidies Office in Prakung, where the incident occurred, reimbursed his loss."

"My God!" I felt within myself, as the meeting broke up for the day. "The poor Laian is owned by the State body and soul."

8

Friday was another one of those evenings for friendship . . . for wine . . . for the spirit. Thak was host at the famous Ehahal, with all the members of the Cabinet and the National Adjudication Panel present. I was the guest of honor.

The banquet began with a toast by Thak: "To the best of health and long life of the only non-Laian who shared his last franc with a struggling member of the Chianglai underground during its darkest days—to G. H.!" His associates joined with gusto: "To G. H.!" I was deeply touched, having learned during the cocktail hour before dinner that Thak had often recounted our difficult days together in Paris and that he had made me into some sort of a hero for the children by relating the incident of my secretly selling my gold watch in order to buy medicine for him while he was sick in bed. I was so moved that all I could do in responding was: "To Chianglai!" To which everyone repeated: "To Chianglai!"

Then there was a toast to each of the eleven new dishes that were served in succession, a toast by each of the ten men around a table to each other individually, and in return. I counted thirty one glasses of wine at dinner alone. They were on the small side, but still thirty one! We enjoyed a rare combination of exotic dishes. Have space for the description of only one—*oyster à la Laiese*. Large precooked sun dried oyster; re-soaked overnight in water; sliced lengthwise like a bun; filled with seasoned paste of fish meat, with chopped ham, chicken, water chestnut, and thin strips of bamboo shoot, flavored with the favorite Laian sauce called *nuoc yeou*, sugar, salt, and pepper; wrapped in pig mesentery; dipped in scrambled egg; rolled in ground crackers; deep fat fried in chicken fat. The individual pieces were artistically arranged with sprigs of parsley, so that they rose out of the large green plate like a majestic mountain in miniature with wind-blown pine trees jutting between the boulders on the steep face.

I had a difficult time falling asleep. I could not reconcile in my mind how the fanatics I had envisioned operating the kind of dictatorial government described in today's briefings could possibly have been the very same people with whom I had spent one of the warmest evenings in my life. I must have been mellowed by too much wine.

9

The first day of the weekend sightseeing consisted of the usual drive around the downtown area of Terkung, looking at public monuments, strolling down the promenade, stopping at a sidewalk café, shopping for souvenirs, taking in a museum. Having seen hundreds of cities and been on scores of Cooke's, Grayline, and what-not tours, I was somewhat blasé about the affair. Thak's company was most enjoyable, as usual, and the rest served as good an enabling context as any— so I felt. As the hours wore on, I began to sense a pervading something in everything I was witnessing. Couldn't put my finger on it. I wondered whether it was what Nam was talking about the other night. Yet it was too vague for me to phrase a meaningful question to be put to Thak. So I decided not to think anymore and let the Laian surroundings soak in as they will. Of a sudden, everything became so *sympatico*!

The second day was spent riding in an open horse carriage through the Central National Park, which covers the northern three fifths of the capital, together with some boating and hiking. No engines of any kind are permitted in the park—not even power mowers. We approached the main gate just as the sun was setting behind the canopy of 400-foot *Dipterocarpus* with their straight white trunks rising a hundred feet without cross branches. Nestled against the nearby stands of orchid trees with their large symmetrical flowers and ornamental markings and crape myrtle's with their terminal clusters of lavender, was the monument of Keikitran and Eleevan. In the center sat a powerful man, stroking the forehead of a cat with a squashed right paw. A bird and a goat were standing next to them. In the background was a semicircle of saddened birds and animals and drooping shrubbery and trees.

"If you can absorb the spirit behind that assemblage in bronze," said Thak almost inaudibly, "you will grasp—how do you Americans put it?—yes, what makes Chianglai tick." "Who is . . ." I started to ask. But it was evident that Thak was talking more to himself than to me. So I decided not to disturb his meditations of the moment and postponed the question for another day.

A Community at the Shore

PRAKUNG

10

Early Monday, our piper cub touched down on a dirt strip, paralleling a long stretch of wide sandy beach. A crowd of about five hundred stood waving at the other end. An elderly man came forward, smiled, bowed, and said: "Welcome to our humble Community of Prakung, my most worthy Elder Brother." The Senior Community Administrator then introduced me to members of his Cabinet. I waved to the friendly people as we walked toward a small pavilion nearby. Wooden pillars and floors, freshly painted, thatched roof.

During tea and sweets, Administrator Olunol assured me that it would be a great honor for himself and his fellow residents if I would think of Prakung as my own home, at least while I am here and hopefully long after I leave, and do whatever pleases me. "What is your honorable pleasure, my most worthy Elder Brother?" I replied that I would like to learn something about how a community operates, what its senior citizens felt to be the principal goals and problems of Prakung, and most importantly, to get to know the people. He seemed particularly pleased with my reference to the people. "As my most worthy Elder Brother says, the people are most important." With that, our agenda was set spending the rest of the day meeting at random with the people in their everyday activities, allotting tomorrow morning to visits to a school, a Catholic church, and a Buddhist wat, and ending with a short briefing in his office in the afternoon covering governmental operations and questions and answers.

"My car and chauffeur are at your disposal. Your aide, Paalol, was born and raised in Prakung and still has many friends living here. He will be able to show you around very nicely. I believe your visits with the people would be more spontaneous if none of the officials would go along. Judging from your expressions, I believe you would prefer such an arrangement. Does this meet with your wishes? Very good. Paalol can phone me during the afternoon so that we can modify the agenda if indicated." We shook hands all around. My aide and I drove off in Olunol's old Citroën.

11

The natives seem to go about their rounds at a steady pace. Nobody loafing yet nobody hustling. Everybody to whom we spoke appeared pleased to engage in light banter or serious conversation as the case may be. There was not the slight indication of annoyance at being interrupted. There was no detectable anxiety about anything.

A 68-year old man planting seedlings along the side of the road—he works part-time in a plant conservation project sponsored by the Old Age Activities Bureau; a shopkeeper with a family business of fine carvings in native hardwoods—an art handed down in his family for generations; a young couple spending their four-day May festival holiday at the beach; Paalol's old friends at the farm cooperative whose lunch of salted giant sea perch, white cabbage, rice, and bananas we shared—each person was refreshing in his own way, but everyone was so genuinely warm and brotherly. A little boy with a kitten, black all over but tipped with white at the chin and paws and with white splashes at the front of the neck, chest, and abdomen, bashfully followed us and after several blocks edged up to Paalol and exchanged a few sentences in Laiese. He then stood back with what appeared to me to be an expression of loving gratitude, as I smiled at him and walked on.

The jovial naturalness of these people I have yet to meet elsewhere. When I am around them, I feel so much at ease not only with them but, strangely so, with myself as well.

12

"What did you and the youngster talk about?" I casually queried my aide just to make conversation. "Something he learned in school," replied Paalol with a faint but noticeable blush, and left it at that. My reporter's instinct was aroused—there's something significant there someplace. I was determined to find out. "What *specifically* did he learn in school?"

"It's a story about a white brother who saved the life of a Laian brother—a very important Laian brother, whom we all deeply love." I started to feel a little lumpiness in my throat, as Paalol decided to tell all. "The boy asked me whether or not you are the good brother from far away who gave everything he had to do it." "And . . . what . . . did . . . you say?" "I said, yes, you are the very kind brother who saved Brother Thak's life."

I turned my head to hide the tears welling up in my eyes.

13

Another one of those evenings for friendship . . . for wine . . . for the spirit. But this time it was indeed trans-socialist! As many people attended the community feast as the produce exchange hall could hold. It was cleaned out for the occasion since it was the largest building in the area. The senior government officials and a thousand others drawn by lot were invited.

The Senior Community Administrator made a short statement to the effect that they were exceedingly glad that I was able to join them in a simple family dinner. This was followed by a loud chorus of "Welcome!" from the rest. The food represented the best produced by the farm cooperative: pork sausages, chicken pot-roasted in *nuoc yeou*, cuttlefish fish with bamboo shoots and mushrooms, duck-omelet with crabmeat and chives, vegetables, rice, mangosteen, and *vin ordinaire*. The feast took the women guests two days to prepare. The men pitched in during their off-hours. The educational highlight for me was the game of *menagee*, which went on at practically all of the tables throughout the evening. Two men stood across each other at the same table, drew back their right arms, then extended it, putting out a number of fingers and at the same time calling out in quaint and poetic phrases what they respectively thought to be the sum of the total number of fingers. The arms darted back and forth progressively faster, the words more eloquent and literary, and the voices more sing-songing and louder until one of the pair guessed right. Then a burst of laughter from the rapt onlookers. And of all things, the *loser* would drink a glass of wine.

At the close of the festivities I counted no less than a hundred good losers wobbling out of the hall amid the understanding chuckle of their friends and relatives. About ten of them could hardly get off the ground. We packed as many into our Citroën as we could at one time. After four round trips, we finally bid the last of the *menagee* players good-night at four in the morning.

14

During our visit to the local General School on Tuesday morning, the Principal described the Laian views on education. Education is considered a lifetime process and therefore everyone is expected to be personally responsible for his own continued development, since he is the only person who can follow his growth over a long period. The General School combines our Elementary and High Schools, compressed into a total of nine years. Every Laian is required to complete it. The main purpose of the General School is to inculcate a sense of wholesome living in the students, a self-reliant confidence that in the goodness of man, the heritage of Chianglai, and the strength of their common endeavors, he, his fellow men, and his descendants will achieve satisfying lives. An important, though clearly secondary aim is to impart the elementary knowledge of reading, writing, and technics. Arts, especially religion and morals, are felt to be a personal matter and the responsibility of the family. The community schools do offer art classes, but these are usually handled after school hours and on Saturdays. The churches similarly provide instructions in religion and morals.

The Principal has complete authority over the students, as long as they are on the campus. He is first of all expected to be a father in being responsible for their character; then secondly, a mentor in being responsible for their knowledge. No rule exists restricting his actions as far as discipline is concerned. However, it has been extremely rare that a Principal in Prakung has been known to raise his voice or lay his hands upon a student. Such an act would be interpreted as failure on the part of the teacher, the parents, or both. The Principal is expected to have resolved the situation long before it reaches such a stage.

We were finally taken on a tour of the school. Buildings were furnished spartan fashion: old wooden chairs, few pictures here and there, but everything clean and neatly in order. We then sat briefly in a class on literature in the sixth grade. The students appear eager and lively but well behaved. One of them was reciting a poem, entitled "Watering Our Land," by the twentieth-century patriot, Melechit:

> Lone elephant in chains clanging,
> Overpower'd by conqueror's herd.
> Taught hiss of asp, his trumpeting
> Wheezes like frail consumptive bird.

> Ancestors, grandsons! Ought I
> Seek success with groveling hand,
> Or for Chianglai, the foe defy?
> Let my blood water our land.

15

After leaving the school, we stopped by a little clearing and watched a game that I've never seen before. The players seemed to be trying to keep something afloat by taking turns kicking it. Paalol told me it was the national sport of *Naloeen* (Flying swallow). Other popular sports in Chianglai include table tennis, cross-country marathon, and water-buffalo racing through a hundred yards of rice paddies. Contests involving intentional body contacts of a potentially injurious nature, such as boxing and American football, are prohibited. Those requiring costly outlays, such as polo and auto-racing, are discouraged.

In *Naloeen* two teams of four persons each stand on opposite sides of net five feet above the ground in a field, 18 by 36 feet in dimensions. Something like a badminton shuttlecock, called the swallow, is used. The base is made up of a flat sponge rubber disc, two and a half inches in diameter and three—eighths inch thick. The top side is feathered so that the swallow floats downwards with the disc in a horizontal position. The object is to get the swallow over the net in three passes or less, as in volleyball. The side which fails to keep it flying has a dead swallow on its hands and loses a point, Twenty points win a set and two sets a game. Only the foot below the ankle is permitted to touch the flying swallow. The average person usually resorts to a cross-kick hitting it with the side of the foot above the instep. At times he may employ a forward-upward motion, using the toes. The masters of the sport, however, are skilled in a variety of techniques. The best players are able to flip a back somersault and while upside down in mid-air, slam the swallow over the net with a swift kick or bluff the opponents with a quick flick.

Since the next two persons on the docket were able to speak English, my aide spent the rest of the morning with his old parents.

16

Father McConnaughy hailed me with a hearty Irish greeting. An impressive six-footer of sixty. His parish numbers two hundred regular communicants and another four hundred of what he jokingly calls "Associate Catholics." He had always been close to the natives and they to him. He had endeared himself to them, non-Catholics and Catholics alike, for his fierce defense of the local people, whether it be against the political or the former ecclesiastical authorities.

"Did the disruption of your financial and institutional ties to Rome hinder you much in your mission?" I came to the point, seeing that Father Mac, as the parishioners call him, grew up in Boston and understood the American directness. "Well, it depends upon what you mean by hindering," he was equally frank. "It was pretty tough sledding at the beginning. Nobody had any money at all. The loans I used to float from the Bishop or the Pope were not available. Today we are able to get indirect subsidies from the State and things don't look too bad as you can see. We have a pretty little church and a fine congregation. You won't find more deeply religious people anywhere. I'm not just talking about Catholics, but the other church-goers as well. Even the local brand of agnostics is not the repugnant intellectuals with their cynical superiority that you find back in the States. The local agnostics seem to be religious in their own way. At times, I'm not sure that they are *really* agnostics, because of their extreme sensitivity to the inexpressible. But by the conventional definitions, I suppose we'll have to classify them as agnostics. I don't believe there are any atheists in Chianglai. Anyway the Laians are first-rate, religion or no religion. Since I'm not much of an empire builder, I'm perfectly contented with preaching the Gospel in the way I'm doing. As a matter of fact, I don't have to hassle with all those nitpicking characters in the former Bishop's secretariat anymore and I don't have to read all of those Curia regulations. Quite a relief, you know. Bureaucrats are the same everywhere. And Rome's no exception. I continue to receive the encyclicals and all that, of course, and I follow them meticulously. I do happen to be one of those old-fashioned priests who believe in celibacy, infallibility of the Pope, and all that, although I *do* love that wine—that wonderful tasting stuff, *mei jiu*. Have you tried some?"

"How about the moral leadership of the Church in Chianglai?" I pressed on. "Political power? Wiped out—gone," he came right to the point. "Monks and ministers are allowed to preach to their hearts' content, so long as it pertains to personal morality, their own beliefs in God, the relationships within the family, and behavior that raises the personal goodness. When it comes to social relationships outside the family, however, that is where the religious preachers have to be very careful. I have no difficulty recognizing the wavering line of demarcation, because I appreciate the underlying philosophy. But it is very fuzzy for the folks back stateside. Anyone is permitted, even encouraged, to discuss the proper relationships of one man with another. But the moment you begin to attach a compulsion of any kind to obeying your statements, that's when the government steps in and say: 'Uh, uh! That's *my* balliwick.' Compulsion by sentencing a person to jail, taking away his money, firing him from his job, threatening with blackmail or eternal hellfire, enticing him with money or heaven—all these belong to the same genre. They are all compulsions regulating society. The people should not have two bosses. Only the people's deputies, elected by the people and guided by the people, can do that. No outsiders, no self-appointed person—no one, not elected by the people—is going to order them around. So far, this hasn't been too bad from my personal standpoint. I've never found any moral doctrine that I would like to preach that is contrary to the laws of the land. And besides I go easy on that theme of reward-and-punishment-after death, which is the bread-and-butter of most churches, as you know. Here though, it seems as if the people would just as soon do something because it is supposed to be right. As to what I would do if the government comes out with something like birth control or abortion, I don't know. But—knock wood—that seems rather unlikely during my lifetime." He thought for a few seconds. "But this does not mean that Catholicism will be gradually squeezed out of this part of the world. The little seedling of faith that I keep watering in this lovely pasture will blossom out again one of these days when the conditions are favorable again. Our Mother Church has been around a long time—much longer than this twenty-three-year-old government. With the Grace of God, we'll outwit and outlive them all!" He winked at me with a broad grin as I got up to hurry to my next interview.

17

Abbot Minh was waiting in front of Prakung's largest wat, when I arrived forty-five minutes late. The pagoda was built a hundred and fifty years ago. The ornate spires and gold-leafed statues reflected the glitter of the former days of religious preeminence. Minh himself had come from a wealthy family, graduated from the Sorbonne, and traveled widely when he was young. He knows about half a dozen languages and still keeps up with the daily *Le Figaro* and occasional issues of the London *Times* and the Manchester *Guardian*. Of all the religious leaders in Chianglai, he is the most respected.

Did he think that the religious spirit of people in general is on the decline, I solicited his opinion over a cup of tea. "No and yes." He felt that the religious spirit of people in general—which he would approximate as a sharing among the living, the "livinged," and the "living-to-come"—is not disappearing. "To say that is is like saying that one's life is disappearing. Both spirits are intrinsic to the living. Their presence is not determined by the camouflage or the suppression that may be exercised over their manifestations. Regrettably, there has been much twisting, bending, and hiding over the centuries. Instead of letting that Sharingness be and being in it as it is to be, however, religious leaders throughout history have been trying to get their followers to see and recognize it in the same way they see and recognize a chief of police, a boss, or a father. These efforts always seem to elicit ready responses. Religion was made easier to grasp, like being immediately on the right side of the chief of police, the boss, or the father. The militant religions then made things still easier by converting this Sharingness to something concrete. It became God and man became His favorite creature. But by so doing, the Sharingness with plants and animals were simplified away. Man's vanity was satisfied and he liked being told of his superior fly over the rest of the earthly sharers. The succeeding generation of religious leaders, trying to better their predecessors, made it still easier by stipulating explicit commandments, explicit prayers and explicit places for communing with God. Still more of the Sharingness became simplified away. Before long, men sensed that they had become self-alienated from the Sharingness which is intrinsically part of themselves. They became dissatisfied with—what's the currently popular American expression? yes, simplistic—with the simplistic abstractions. The so-called decline in religious spirit throughout the world today is actually the feeling for Sharingness pushing through the artificial layers of suppression. People are not questioning this Sharingness but questioning their faith in conventions designed for the spiritually lazy. They in fact are seeking a return to their true belonging."

Did he think that his own church will play a leading role in the revival of this Sharingness? "I don't know," he confessed in modest candor. "We ourselves—the respected elders of our own religion—we also have embroidered our own practices. We too have simplified the Sharingness away through appealing facsimiles. Even though our religion is not aggressively missionizing by nature, nevertheless our dominant position in certain regions has made some of us—myself included, I fear—a little proud in the conviction that we are at least a little more acquainted with *the* truth than others. We forget that the very essence of Sharingness denies priority to any one in particular. So in answer to your question, we hope to do our part by first righting our own selves. We do not feel inclined to lead a crusade for the revival of the so-called true spirit. But we will be pleased to share our experience with others, so that we may mutually benefit by heightened awareness of the Sharingness, which binds us all together."

18

As I left the Abbot, my own smug attitude exhibited during Naaouk's briefing at Terkung came to mind. Yes, *I* knew *the* truth. No question about it, I *was* arrogant. Perhaps, *still* am. In his unwitting way, the Abbot taught me my first very important lesson in Chianglai. I hope I'll never forget it.

This Sharingness . . . it's so vague.

Yet, coming to think of it . . . so is God Himself.

19

At lunch, the Senior Community Administrator showed considerable interest in learning about the American people. He said that he had heard much about American democracy and has studied the writings of Thomas Jefferson and Ralph Waldo Emerson with great admiration. He mentioned that the people of Prakung refer to America as the Golden Valley, where everyone is wealthy with a television in every home and two cars in every front yard. "How do you Americans manage your government, such that everybody is so comfortable and happy? Can you tell me some of the things that we are doing wrong here in Prakung so that our people can come a trifle closer to the good life of your brethren in America?" he asked with eager anticipation.

When I told him that there are many unemployed people in America, he was surprised. When I added that some even starve from time to time and go naked, he was shocked. But then he quickly composed himself and apologized for failing to notice that it was only courteous modesty expressing self-deprecation on the part of his most worthy Elder Brother.

I decided not to disillusion the old gentleman and abruptly changed the subject.

20

"Sir," I rechanneled his trend of thought, "I have been much impressed with how happy *your* brethren are here in Prakung. You must work very hard to bring this about. On what particular aspect do you spend most of your energies?" As he bit the bait and started to reply, I heaved a sigh of relief. I could imagine how he would have keeled over had we gotten around to the truth about medical care and mental illness in America.

"You are so kind in your generous remarks, most worthy Elder Brother," he demurred, insisting that he has very little to do with it. "Happiness comes primarily from within the individual. Yet the individual is really the confluence of many, many peoples who lived before him and who are living today. The happiness which springs from himself has to be enlivened by the rest of Nature. If everyone remains sensitive to this kindredness, a tradition conducive to human joyfulness evolves. The longer it is nourished, the deeper it grows and the more imperturbable it stands in the face of the normal hardships that arises from day to day." The Administrator spends most of his time, therefore, trying to instill this sense of belonging in the people, as expressed in concrete fashion in their work and play, their gladness and suffering, their communal activities and personal lives. He does not lecture or preach. He leads by putting forth examples of his own, praising those who are doing well in this regard, comforting those who feel miserable in their failures, and gently—very gently—nudging them in the right direction. All this, he agreed, takes great patience. There are no short cuts.

His thesis sounded very familiar. "Do you belong to Abbot Minh's Pagoda?" I made a guess. "I am afraid that I am not familiar with the teachings of the highly respected Abbot, most worthy Elder Brother," he confessed. "You see, I am an agnostic."

21

The formal briefing that afternoon at the Community Headquarters covered the same general outline of the operations of a community as was presented in Terkung, except in greater detail. I was particularly intrigued with their views and programs on radio and television.

I opened the question period with: "Why is radio and television put under the Administrator for Education, instead of the Administrator for Community Enterprises or Personal Well-Being?" In his exposition, the briefer called attention to the fact that it is listed in the first position under the Administrator for Education. Radio and television are considered the primary means of education for the country, because they can reach the entire nation simultaneously. They are among the few means for family and community group instruction. Social instruction, then, can best be attained by radio and television, as contrasted to individual education best performed by the schools, and peer group education by institutions of employment, worship, and the like. It is for this reason that education has been designated as the primary function of radio and television. Half of their budgets are devoted directly to educational programs. Next in importance comes information and cultural enrichment, although these too can be regarded as education. Entertainment enjoys a relatively low emphasis on radio and television.

"Does this mean that leisure and entertainment are de-emphasized in Chianglai?" "On the contrary," the briefer reassured me. "Leisure is considered essential for the good life. It is a right guarded by long tradition. Even elephants working in the teak forests are given a four-month vacation every year. But we encourage the participatory kind of leisure and the person-to-person type of entertainment, such a concert, a play, and outdoor sports. We discourage the less directly personal variety, such as movies, radio, and television. Each time you insert an inanimate device between two human beings, somehow the human warmth does not get through. Human warmth is what makes for a wholesome society. If the people learn to exist without it, then the society turns cold. We try to keep that uppermost in our minds, not only in entertainment but in everything else we do."

22

"Where does the power of the government come from?" I posed a leading question. "From the people," came the expected cliché. "Can you tell me how this is attained in your form of government?"

The briefer carried on in his personable manner, without apparently recognizing the intended challenge. "Every person above sixteen is required to vote in the elections for the Citizens' Deputies, This is the first step in their exercise of power. But that is not all. A vote of confidence is held midway through the term of office. If the incumbent receives less than sixty per cent of the votes, he is expected to resign his membership in the Community Chamber of Deputies and the Chairman will appoint someone else to complete the unfilled term of office. The same secret vote of confidence is held by the Community Chambers with respect to their own representatives to the Regional Chamber and the Chairman of the Community Chamber. The Regional Chambers and the National Chamber go through an analogous vote of confidence. In this way, there is no question in anyone's mind that the Deputies are in fact servants of the people. After all, to be lacking the necessary vote of confidence is a shame most people would dread. Fortunately so far, the lowest vote of confidence registered in the thirteen years of experience is sixty-six per cent. Furthermore, since the elected officials are restricted to a single term and a half in the same echelon there is a greater distribution of opportunity to actually wield power among the citizens. Finally, the electoral subdivisions are of such a small geographical area or population that the Deputies are known personally to the majority of the older citizens or their immediate friends and many of the younger voters and even children. In other words, the people are voting for a real person whose behavior they have personally observed for many years in actual situations.

"There is also direct participation in the legislative process itself. A referendum is held on major issues twice a year. Each issue is clearly delineated and the available options given, on which the opinion of the people is solicited. The Deputies are not necessarily bound by the option receiving the highest vote. But their explanations for departures need to be very convincing. Again every one above sixteen is required to vote."

23

With the hour remaining before our scheduled flight time, I wanted to get some better idea of the intriguing sounding Cabinet position of Administrator for Personal Well-Being. So I dropped in on him unannounced. He jumped out his chair when I showed up and was very pleased to see me. He felt it a great honor that I should regard his office worthy of my limited time.

"You may say that my principal concern is two-fold," he summarized the functions of his office. "The first is to study what makes for a good life as a whole. How excesses or deficiencies in one phase affects well-being in another. How a person craves various satisfactions at different stages of his life and how the means are made available and feasible to meet them at the time and place of need, This planning is done as a Special Assistant to the Senior Community Administrator.

"The Second concern of my group is the operational responsibility for some of the programs related to the psychic aspects of well-being. We do not regard the arts, sports, music, theater, and the like as secondary luxuries to the material, biological, and even educational requirements of man. They are inseparable elements of enriched living. As a result, we try to be as proficient in meeting the requirements in these activities as we do in medicine and agriculture. After all, what is more important than the cultural expressions of one's way of life?"

24

At that point the aide entered somewhat excited and stated that we have to be at the air strip forty-five minutes ahead of schedule because of unforeseen circumstances. I shook the Administrator's hand and departed. Senior Administrator Olunol was waiting in the car to accompany us to the plane. As we approached the airfield, I saw a crowd of about five thousand gathered there before a hastily improvised platform. The Senior Administrator introduced me to one of the men, a Brother Akanna, whom I recognized as the most vigorous *menagee* player at the community feast the other night. Next to him stood the proprietor of the little carving shop, with whom I had passed a very pleasant hour the other afternoon. The two of them led me up to the platform. I motioned to Olunol to come along, but he insisted on staying back.

"Most honorable Elder Brother," Akanna commenced. "You have come from far away. You have shaken our hands. You have talked with us. You have eaten with us when we were happy. You have taken us home when we were sick. We have come to like you. We now know that men far away can also be brothers, because we now have one ourselves. We thank you for this. Your brothers here in Prakung would like to present you with a little gift. This gift was made from an old tree grown right here in Prakung. The tree was over four hundred years old. The work was done by Loianol here. Loinaol's ancestors have lived here for a thousand years, ever since Prakung was founded. We wish you *bon voyage!*" There was a loud and sustained cheer as he handed me a beautiful carving of a plant and animal grouping. I was too overwhelmed for words. I bowed to Akanna, then to Loianol, then to Olunol, and then to the people, I waved as I stumbled off the platform, walked reluctantly to the plane, slowly shook the Senior Administrator's hand, bowed again—this time deeply and deeply felt—to my brethren of Prakung, and stepped hesitatingly into the Piper Cub.

As the plane taxied into position for takeoff and began to speed down the runway, I peered out the window for one last look. There at the edge of the multitude stood a little boy waving, with a kitten at his side, black all over but tipped with white at the chin and paws and with white splashes at the front of the neck, chest, and abdomen.

Regional Headquarters in the Foothills

SAIKUNG

25

The Senior Regional Administrator greeted us upon our arrival at Saikung late Tuesday. We were invited to stay at his guest house and to relax with him that evening. While we were unpacking, my aide gave me a quick rundown on Administrator Nahanu's background—a young brilliant executive. But the warmest praise was reserved for the 76-year-old father, who was to join us for dinner. He is respected as one of the wisest men in Chianglai. Men come from all the country to seek his advice.

Dinner was rather simple but quite tasty. A five-course affair with rice and some wine. At the propitious moment in our after-dinner conversation I popped my usual question for occasions of this kind. What was his chief personal concern as Senior Regional Administrator? He acknowledged that he has no difficulty identifying it, although he felt that he was far from a satisfactory performance. "I spend much time attempting to maintain an optimal balance between progress and serenity for the people as a whole. What is the appropriate pace of change, so that it can be assimilated in a harmonious continuum with our own identities? On the one hand, we are a materially underdeveloped country trying to catch up. Change is thrusting itself upon us from all sides. Our younger managers are impatient with what they feel to be a terrible waste of manpower. If given full rein they can easily double or even triple their factory output in many cases. On the other hand, the good life of our people rests on a measured pace in all things. We cannot be gentle and kind if we are dashing about all the time. We would wear everybody out in the process, including ourselves. Anxiety will gloom the land. This might not have been such a strong concern of mine, of course, had I not been brought up to place great value on moderation and on compassion. It might not have commanded such central attention on the part of our national leaders had they been willing to place a lower importance on a satisfying life for *every* Laian and had they been willing to sacrifice a percentage of the people here and there for the sake of a more abundant material affluence for the bulk of the population or the nation as a whole."

Does he think that he and his associates will succeed in resisting the world-wide trend of materialism and depersonalization? He thought for a few seconds and turned to his father for an opinion. "I do not believe the leaders will succeed in stopping this wave from engulfing Chianglai in the next forty years," the father slowly expressed his reservations. "The cultural pendulum swings continuously. Currently, it is drifting away from our old tradition—that of gentle humanness. It will go past the point of optimal balance to the other extreme of aggressive materialism. But it will come back again after the evil has spent itself. The crucial question is this: When the pendulum does return will the people of Chianglai be able to bring this experience of suffering and the wisdom that should issue from such tribulations—will they be able to bring it into the mainstream of our Laian heritage and ascend to a higher plateau of human excellence? The elders and the leaders would not have defaulted because they have not stopped the natural swings of the cultural pendulum. They would have failed if they have not bred a sturdy stock that makes it possible for the future generations to reach a fuller realization of good living with each swing of the pendulum. If they fail in this way, the descendants will be subjected to an aimless and endless to-and-fro, marking time on a reversing treadmill, ever moving faster, now in one direction, now in the opposite, yet always getting nowhere—an eternal pointless befuddlement. It is this befuddlement that generates much of the present anxiety of meaninglessness and emptiness in many lives. When the people have faith in their continued growth in basic values and recognize the essential strands that must remain unbroken, no matter what may be the enticements of expediency and temporary alleviation of pain, then they will be patient, persevering, and optimistic in the midst of adversity. I believe the leaders in Chianglai are giving the people this abidingness. In this way, I say they are successful in resisting the current wave of materialism and depersonalization."

26

On Wednesday morning, the official orientation on regional activities was given by the Chief of the Regional Planning Panel. It was typical for briefings of this kind—organization charts, functions, goals, accomplishments, problems. The briefer struck me as an unusually gifted person in some way that I couldn't quite fathom, although there was nothing special that he had said that would suggest any extraordinary talent on his part. So I decided to probe his own field of specialty—planning—instead of becoming bored with the usual bureaucratic details of administration. "Quite apart from the paper priorities, guidance documents from topside, and the like," I asked, "how do you go about deciding where to start in planning? Is there a standard step-by-step procedure for planners in Chianglai?"

"No, there are no set procedures on how to do planning. There are prescribed formats and procedures only for promulgating the results of planning. The latter are necessary so that the translations into actual operating programs can proceed smoothly," he quietly brought out. Then slowly: "But as to how one goes about planning itself is difficult to say. It is somewhat like asking how one goes about being creative. Come to think of it, planning itself is a form of creativity. I suppose the approach varies from person to person, context to context. It probably depends even upon the kind of leaps over factual voids one is usually compelled to make. I really haven't sat down and tried to analyze how I myself went about it until you raised the question just now. . . ."

"In my own case, usually," he proceeded even more slowly than before, "usually I begin by simply talking to many individuals about anything that may possibly be relevant to the general area under consideration . . . and about subject matter that may not appear to be so . . . no thinking particularly, just talking. At the same time I do a lot of reading, sightseeing . . . Still no thinking, no analyzing—just reading, sightseeing. I'd sit and reflect—muse is a more descriptive word—but not try to effect any closure at the time. I'd then talk some more, read some more, sightsee some more, muse some more. Then one day, the completely integrated outline of the plan would burst into light and almost force itself into my vision, as it were. All I need to do then is to flesh out the details. There was never an identifiable starting point. The plan arrived whole. I suppose this may be one of the symbolism's behind Minerva emerging fully matured from the head of Jupiter."

27

It was quite a drive to the Saikung University, which is located in the suburbs on the other side of town. Along the way we passed several men walking along the side of the road with a pole over the shoulder at each end of which was a ten gallon cylindrical container. The aide identified them as traveling noodle restaurants. "Let's have some for lunch from the next fellow," I suggested.

We stopped. The aide ordered three bowls for us and the driver. The vendor placed his containers on the ground and removed the lids. Taking some noodles from one can, he placed them into the boiling water above a brazier of hot coals in the other can for a few minutes. He then dished them out with some of the hot water. A teaspoonful of dehydrated chicken flavoring was sprinkled into the bowl and the contents stirred with a pair of chopsticks. Finally he carefully counted out four thin slices of barbecued pork and a sprig of parsley and neatly arranged them on top. The bowls were placed on the recovered cans. Unfolding little stools at the side, he gestured that luncheon was served and stood patiently by waiting for us to finish.

Engaging him in conversation, I learned that he is an overseas Cantonese. His wife prepares the ingredients at home and he peddles the noodles as a private entrepreneur. He chooses to do this rather than work in the government factories because he would make about sixty per cent more income this way. It appears that there are no Laians in this line of business. After we parted, I turned to my aide: "Why not?" He ascribed it to the fact that Laians are not ambitious by nature. "They are far more contented than even the Chinese!" he said in a tone of pride.

28

The Provost of the University was a most articulate person, very sure of himself, quite atypical of the Laians I've met so far. He was most pleasant otherwise, and I believe, at bottom, just as human-hearted as the rest. I suspect that he must be hard driven subconsciously to show himself as a leading scholar in the face of the other highly renowned teachers on the campus. Yet his outspokenness was refreshing to me, after the last week of self-effacing reservations on the part of the other Laians.

The curriculum is divided into three series. These are: Living, Ecology, and Heritage. Every student is required to enroll in a minimum of courses in each of the three series. The details were to be covered by the senior teachers in each of the series when I visit them later in the day. Those students who wish to proceed to the professional schools will take an examination at the end of two years. If they pass, they are accepted and can expect to graduate in three additional years. If they choose not to do so, they can expect to complete the university degree in another year, making it three in all. Masters or Doctorates are neither awarded nor recognized in Chlanglai. The national policy is to raise the educational level of everybody in the country to a minimum standard as rapidly as possible before siphoning off funds for further intellectual development of a relative few. The question of advanced degrees will be reexamined in ten years. Perhaps Chianglai will follow the rest of the world and reinstate the practice at that time. But it may be that the intervening experience will show that advanced degrees are not contributory as such to the welfare of the country or the good life of the people. "I believe the latter will turn out to be the case," prophesied the Provost, who has a Ph.D. in mechanics from Brooklyn Poly himself.

"As far as grades are concerned," he mounted the rostrum again, "we give none. Our thinking is that since every graduate gets a job anyway, and since everyone begins at approximately the same starting salary, there is no need for the university to act as an evaluation device for the determination of the differential starting salaries as practiced in some of the other countries. I understand that the Bell Laboratories in your countries recruit graduates only from those making grades in the upper ten per cent in engineering schools. In Chianglai, the supervisors at work evaluate the performance worthiness of the individual for promotion. The past grades don't mean a thing. It's what you do on the job that counts. Why then give grades? Some may argue that they are needed as incentives for the students. But if grades can't even buy you a cup of coffee, then what kind of incentive is it? To show up your fellow students competitively? This is hardly a worthy motivation. What we try to do is to assist each student, and I would like to emphasize the word *assist* for the student is expected to be his own prime mover to better himself, to develop his potentialities to the maximum within the time available and resources allotted. The rest is up to him to show what he can do for society when he is called upon to do so after graduation. And since he won't have grades *then*, he might as well get used to not having it *now*."

29

The Senior Teacher of the Living Series was the antithesis of the Provost—modest, understanding, and natural. A better exemplar of lofty living is hard to find anywhere. "What we try to offer," he pointed out in perfect Oxford English, "is a medley of exposures—I should emphasize that we do not give lectures, but only provide exposures—to impart a quickening sense of the living." To him that is the core of a meaningful education—a quickening sense of life. The rest is mechanical and intellectual auxiliaries.

The disciplines of esthetics, psychiatry, philosophy, human physiology, and the like are subsumed under one course, called "Personal Well-Being." Just as a beautiful piece of music can be any combination of infinite variations of the same basic sounds, so can life be made satisfying by the proper blending of even individually discordant notes, when played by themselves under another setting. One listens to the total effect of the musical piece.

If it is pleasing he sits back and enjoys it. If it is not, he may then listen analytically in an attempt to find out what particular facet went "wrong." The analogous approach is used by the Senior Teacher in his exposures. The student is taught first to apprehend life as a whole. Only when he begins to be conversant with this intuitive art, is he then introduced into the analysis of pathologic states, each of which is referred back to the wholesome whole.

But man does not live alone. He lives in the midst of people—he in them and they in him. So here again, the conventional disciplines of ethics, sociology, political science, economics, and the like are subsumed in a single course, entitled "Social Well-Being." "In this case, we begin with the well-being of the society," the Senior Teacher expanded on the theme. "We learn to sense the state of the entire situation or event—neither failing to see the forest for the trees nor letting the canopy obstruct the little shrubs below."

30

"How about the sciences and engineering?" I interrupted. "I'm grateful that you reminded me of this important matter," he continued. "They fall into the third course, entitled 'Supporting Technics', which also includes foreign languages, trades, professions, and the like. The term 'Supporting Technics' had been deliberately chosen to make clear that 'Personal Well-Being' and 'Social Well-Being' constitute the primary goals of education. The rest of the academic activities are supportive of these aims and are judged of worth only insofar as they contribute to their realization."

I then wondered whether he would identify the capstone quality which is being imparted to the students. "It is difficult to capture it in words, since actually it is an indescribable projection of the superior man. It includes not only *what* a person does, but also *how* he does it; not only *what* impact is objectively delivered, but also *how* the impact is felt in the innermost being of the recipient," the professor slowly explained. "If you are compelled to fall back on a single term—more of a reminder, of course, than as a descriptor—I suppose it might be *graciousness*." He then tried to convey its subtle qualities by means of a succession of round-about allusions and stories.

Finally, he sought *our* views in America on graciousness, so that he "might improve his own insight and teaching." I responded that I had never really given the subject any thought. But our Library of Congress contains over fifteen million volumes and pamphlets and I offered to go over the extensive card catalogue upon my return and send him a list of twenty selected books on graciousness. I also mentioned my own collection of three thousand literary excerpts on human behavior, out of which I shall forward copies of the most appropriate ones. He seemed most pleased at the prospect of "learning much from your wise and scholarly brethren" and expressed profuse appreciation.[*]

31

The Senior Teacher in Ecology voiced the *same* conceptual approach to learning. He himself had preferred that there not be a splitting off of Ecology and Heritage from Living. "The more one dissects and breaks down the overall apprehension," he commented, "the harder it becomes to retain the integrity of the man."

He granted, however, that there might have been compelling reasons for the separation of the Ecology and Heritage Series from the Living Series. Chiang-lai feels a need to regain the traditional love of the land and the culture. The people have been under foreign domination on and off for almost two hundred years—seven generations. In order to emphasize the sense of belonging to some-

---

* My letter on graciousness is presented in Appendix IV.

thing of far greater significance than an ephemeral form of local government or a confined acreage of one's own little plot of land, the government had decided to focus special attention to Ecology and Heritage through such an educational means.

The term Ecology, as used locally, does not have the connotation of the "environment" as used in America. There is no separation of man *and* his environment; rather, there is a *fusion* of man and his environment. Ecology represents the study of the ecological entity as a whole. When a given ecological complex appears unfavorable from the standpoint of man, for example, he does not have a prior claim to adjustment on the part of the other elements of the complex. The others have just as much "right" to demand modification of *his* behavior as he has on *theirs*. All are one in Nature. The appreciation of this Oneness and the delicate interrelationships of its diffusions represents the prime academic purpose of the Ecology Series.

32

The Senior Teacher in Heritage, Elder Brother Dibom, was a gracious man of seventy-two with sparse white flowing whiskers. He had been the first Senior Community Administrator of Prakung. While he was there, he had been a close friend of Minh.

There are no pre-set agendas in the Heritage Series. The program is partly tailored to the individual, but largely unstructured. Those who have never associated with peasants, for example, might spend some time on the farms. Those who have not been in a white-collar environment before might spend some time in a government office. The sessions themselves are held in various parts of the surrounding places. The locations are announced ahead of time. Anyone may attend simply by showing up. The attendees are divided into discussions groups of about thirty each. The subject matter evolves from the interests of the gathering. Usually someone mentions an issue or occurrence which strikes him as especially exemplary of what's commendable or otherwise in the evolution of the national character. If it does not strike a responsive chord, it recedes into the background as a passing conversational interest. If it does, then the group joins in an animated exploration of the philosophical meanings and practical ramifications behind the happening, the relationship to the traditional ideologies, the consistencies with government practices and prevailing mores, the possible extensions of the underlying principles, the point of excessive emphasis and its impact upon the preservation of other Laian values, the long-term trajectory of the course of action being initiated, and the like.

All of the senior government officials participate in these sessions on a more or less regular basis—about six times a year on the average. They consider them to be one of their principal ways of keeping touch with the people and of maintaining the proper direction as determined by the most basic of Laian points of reference. That is why it has been said that Elder Brother Dibom is the most influential person on governmental affairs.

33

Most of the professions are taught on the job—including the degree of technical proficiency normally conveyed in our graduate schools. It is incumbent upon the Chief of Adult Education in the Regional Administration to see to it that this part of the development of the worker is not neglected by the management of the various enterprises in their push to exceed the prescribed production quota. There are only two formal professional schools in Chianglai, namely, Medical Welfare and Political Welfare.

The Saikung Medical Welfare University trains medical doctors, with abbreviated courses for nurses, medical technicians, hospital administrators, and medical engineers. In the case of the medical doctors, the usual courses of anatomy, pathology, and other technical disciplines are supplemented with what may be designated as clinical sociology. The undergraduate series on personal well-being is extended to practical measures. The doctor is taught to sense the total state of the patient's well-being and the part that medicine in the limited technical sense plays in it. While he is curing the patient of his physiological or psychological symptoms, the good doctor also refers the patient to the other services bureaus which are equipped to care for the rest of his troubles. The doctor's first question is always: What is the state of well-being of the person as a whole? Then only, does the second question arise: What part can my own specialized skill play? And the third: Who else can help restore his feeling of integrated well-being?

This approach to personal and social problems is being firmly indoctrinated into the young men coming into practice. The medical doctors are not alone in this respect. Ombudsmen, old-age activities officials, ministers, teachers, and executives of all kinds are expected to follow through in a similar way whenever some troubled Laian comes to them for help. One can say that—now I am beginning to sound repetitious—it's getting to be part of their heritage.

34

The Saikung Political Welfare University is especially interesting to me. There are no law schools as such in the country. As a matter of fact, law as practiced in most countries in the West would be regarded as a malignant moral cancer, which if unchecked would destroy the very fiber of the Laian personality in short order. The Provost did not say so in actual words, but I gathered that to be his sentiments. The government is trying desperately to substitute its own concepts for those of uncompromising justice and cunning legalisms left by the foreign conquerors. The Provost believes that the changeover will be completed in about two generations. Everyone is optimistic that this will come about even sooner and nothing seems to be standing in the way. "Our Senior Regional Adjudicator is especially pleased with the progress," he reported. "In his recent commencement address, he encouraged the graduates with his observation that even American jurisprudence is moving in our direction. 'Very soon,' he said, 'the entire world will be following the prestigious American Bar. Men everywhere will come to see the beneficence of our customs.' It was very helpful for us to hear this, of course. Our younger students are greatly influenced by what is happening in your great country and they read your literature avidly."

He then emphasized that it is an art which is being inculcated—the art of enlightening and leading one's fellow men. "This is the most sophisticated of all arts. Most sophisticated, I believe, because the strength to lead must be accompanied with the wisdom to guide and both blended with the humility of service and the love of man and beast—yet, all the time with practical goodness." This is entirely different, he kept repeating, from the technique of ruling. Practically anybody can rule or give orders, especially when backed up by lots of minds and muscles, monies and guns, and rewards and punishments.

How can a deeply felt concern for a fellow man's well-being and an instinctive reasonableness in demands be incorporated into community behavior? How can elasticity in constraints be maintained in everyday events so that harmless individual idiosyncrasy can be accommodated? How can the strong, as a matter of reflex response, lift up the weak who have fallen into misfortune?—these are the points of departure in the curriculum. The procedures for framing Citizens' Prescriptions, the manner of presentation of one's case before the Adjudication Panel, and other technical details are also covered, but only as supporting technics to the purposes described. Such procedural and mechanical matters can be acquired during the student's later apprenticeships after graduation.

35

Nothing was scheduled for the evening. So the aide and I sauntered about town. We turned up a side alley. Both sides were lined with little shacks, barely six feet high. From one of them came the voice of a young mother amusing her giggling infant:

> Rhino walking, rhino walking.
> Clop! Clop! Clop! Clop!
> Egret riding, egret riding.
> Aark! Aark! Aark! Aark!

Outside, women were sprinkling water over the areas before their doors to keep the dust down and tidying up the place with loosely tied bundles of twigs. Up ahead was a cluster of children, noisily gesticulating—now looking down on the ground in a huddle, now comforting a bawling child on the side. We moved quickly to investigate.

It turned to be another replay of one of those perennial crises of children all over the world. The child had dropped his last penny through the iron grill into the bottom of the drain pipe about eight inches below. They parted as we approached. The child stopped crying. Everyone looked at us hopefully. I tugged at the grating. It wouldn't budge, rusted. Sighs of disappointment all around. My face brightened with an idea. The lads were encouraged anew. They watched my every move as I reached over for the broom leaning against the wall, carefully untied the bundle of twigs, selected two of the longest and straightest pieces, stuck them through the grating, slowly fished out the penny chopstick-style, and handed it with a smile to the child.

A triumphal burst of exultation was followed by a yelling scattering of children in all directions heralding our great achievement! The older folks poked their heads out of the shacks up and down the alley to see what was happening. The child with the penny ran overflowing with joy into the outstretched arms of his mother. I carefully retied the broom and placed it back where it had lain. My aide and I took one more glance at the heart-warming scene and resumed our sauntering.

36

Barely had we gone forty yards when we heard footsteps back of us. We turned around and saw a strapping fellow of about a hundred and seventy pounds and five feet nine, which is quite large for a Laian, running after us.

He stopped. Introduced himself as Ikaikor, the father of the child with the penny. He told us that he had never seen his child so happy before and wanted to thank me for it.

"Honorable Elder Brother," he bowed again. "Our family is very poor. Our house is old. Our food is not worthy of Honorable Elder Brother. But we have just set our table for dinner. If you two honorable brethren would share it with our family, it will make this evening one of the most joyful occasions of our lives."

37

We sat on wooden stools, homemade out of packing crates, around a small round table. The meal consisted of steamed catfish seasoned with *nuoc yeou*, sugar, salt, and ginger, cabbage soup, yam, and rice.

The closely knit family included the respected father, the quiet mother who did not say a word all night but stole a grateful glance at me now and then, an eight-year-old son, a six-year-old daughter, and the lad with the penny seated beside me.

The lad didn't eat a thing, save an obliging bite or two, when urged on by his mother's look. From the side of my eyes I could see that he had his attention glued on me throughout the meal. Once in a while he'd nudge right up to me and when I would cast a friendly nod his way, a huge cheerful grin would cover his face from ear to ear.

38

Ikaidor is employed in the local steel works. He is a member of a labor crew, which manhandles the buggies transporting the ingots from the blast furnace to the hot strip mill.

The plant is planning to replace the crew with little locomotives. In preparation for the changeover, he and the other laborers are taking classes at the Adult Education School. Three hours a day during the week are counted against work. The eight hours on Saturdays are on their own.

Ikaidor is learning the technique of welding. After another week of training, he expects to get a promotion and become a welder, joining sheets on the galvanizing line. He has seen where he will be stationed and has met the new superintendent. The job will pay much more; the work will be much easier; the family will be far better off. He is looking forward to it with considerable enthusiasm.

39

As we got up to leave, I could see that Ikaidor was looking around eagerly for something to give me as a memento. But I could also see that there was nothing even remotely suitable in sight.

The little son motioned to his father and whispered something into his ear. The father smiled, nodded his head, and said to me: "My son would like to say something to you, Honorable Elder Brother." I turned to the boy and bent over to hear what he had to say.

He gently reached for my hand, carefully placed the penny in it, ceremoniously closed my fingers over it, and gave me a warm and long hug as if he didn't want to let go. Then he quickly let go and ran to the side of his dad and the whole family bowed together as we bid them goodnight.

40

On Thursday morning we visited the Saikung Armament Works, considered to be the most modern factory in Chianglai. It manufactures some kind of small guided missile for the sea forces. Looks like the American SideWinder, about the same length but only half in diameter.

After a hasty tour of the plant—a typical American layout, having actually been planned by an American electronics company through its French subsidiary—we settled down with the Manager for a discussion of his views on management. He castigated the bureaucrats at Saikung and Terkung headquarters as being excessively idealistic and theoretical. "This talk about brotherhood and the good life for man and all that is fine," he waved his right arm in a wide arc. "But that doesn't get the production out. The sea forces have been putting terrific pressure on me to deliver more of the weapon sub-system into their hands. National Security Priority Triple A and all that. Yet when I take steps to cut out those programs of waste, like personnel development and compulsory vacations—oh yes, if a guy is so inspired that he wants to work instead of taking time off for vacations, why do we have to prevent him from doing so? After all, this is a free country, isn't it? Anyway, as soon as I try to get *really* efficient, I get a directive from some clerk up there to cease and desist. You know, this puts a helluva bind on us shirt-sleeve engineers who have to get the work out!"

His mannerisms and American idioms with a Bostonian accent made me feel quite at home. Later I found out that he was a graduate of M.I.T.

41

We next sat through the tail end of a robbery trial before the Saikung Regional Adjudication Panel, "Did you *really* see Brother Kalaiswa climbing into the window?" the Citizens' Adjudication Counselor (analogous to our defense attorney) directed a question to the principal state witness. "Yes, Brother Counselor." "But judging from where you said you were sitting and the darkness of the night, it would appear very difficult for you to identify the person with any degree of certainty." Then turning to the Regional Adjudication Counselor (analogous to our prosecutor), the Citizens' Adjudication Counselor advanced the possibility to him: "Would you not agree, Brother Counselor?" The latter allowed that might well be the case. Whereupon, the two counselors got together with the three members from the Adjudication Panel and came up with a tentative disposition of the case.

"Before we advance our own proposal, Brother Kalaiswa, do you wish to make any comment on the situation?" the Senior Adjudicator addressed the defendant. "No, Brother Senior Adjudicator." "We have agreed that there is some likelihood that you are innocent of the charge of robbing the Saikung Regional Museum of its jade Buddha. On the other hand, the account of your actions during the course of the evening is far from convincing. Perhaps you refrained from giving us a complete picture for good and personal reasons. Yet, your recent general behavior toward your brethren has not been commendable, especially toward your kind father. We therefore feel that you should spend some time contemplating the true values of life. Instead of the three years initially thought to be appropriate by Brother Regional Counselor, however, we are proposing a year's stay. Do you wish to make any comments before we finalize our judgment?" "No, Brother Senior Adjudicator."

"In that case," pronounced the Senior Adjudicator, "one year at the Indoctrination Center it will be. We wish you well, Brother Kalaiswa."

42

I was still having a hard time getting over the trial, when we entered the Senior Adjudicator's chambers as his guests for lunch. The whole affair seemed so mushy. By the time we sat down, I was so worked up that I launched into an exposition of the vigorous superiority of the American court procedures without any of the niceties which normally accompany polite conversations between strangers.

The Senior Adjudicator could not believe his ears when I described the details of the adversary proceedings in our system of justice, especially when I came to the courtroom practice in which data favorable to your side are selectively exaggerated and those unfavorable are strongly contested even when you know them to be the truth. Enjoying the dramatic effects being created by my revelations, I continued with recent vivid examples of bribing offenders with the offers of lighter sentences if they would testify against their former friends and of legislators compelling people to betray their best friends in a public hearing, and the increasing clever stationing of informants. I showed how no stone is left unturned in the unearthing of evidence against the criminal. At that point his eyes met mine and I realized that I had gone too far.

He dropped his fork with its piece of steak, got up from the table in a daze, and gazed out of the window. "Have I been misleading my Laian students all these years?" he mumbled to himself. "Was what I told them about the leadership of American jurisprudence in bringing the world around to our reasonable and compassionate dispensation of justice an illusion? What will they do when they find out? Insist that justice has *two* sides? That the pursuit of justice must have adversaries? That the ultimate purpose of justice is no longer reconciliation but dissolution? What will the powerful influence of that mighty nation *now* do to the hearts of our young people in Chianglai? Will they come to distrust each other more and more . . . and love each other less and less . . . as time goes on?"

43

The more I think back upon the incident, the more I regretted having brought up the subject of our approach to criminal justice. Originally I thought it would make stimulating conversation. But now, I'm afraid I've ruined his day. That stare in his eyes began to haunt me as I trudged slowly over to the next appointment.

I entered the Internal Peace Officers Headquarters deeply regretting what I had just done. "You go around without the slightest consideration of the delicate sensibilities of other people. You shoot off your blabbering mouth. You tell the world how *you* do it in America. Big deal! You smash their ideals. You trample over them, You scatter your smut. Then you say, 'I'm sorry!' A filthy lot of good *that* does!" I hung my head in shame and sorrow.

The Chief of Internal Peace Officers (analogous to our Chief of Police) bounded out of his office into the reception room with a boisterous welcome. But seeing that I wasn't up to it, he invited me into his office and solicitously inquired whether I was ill. Was there anything he could do for me? Should he call a doctor? At first I didn't say anything. But feeling the need to tell my troubles to somebody, to confess my sins as it were, I recounted the painful episode. He listened with sympathetic silence. When I finished and looked up, I noticed that his own eyes were red and misty. I gathered that he must have realized that he too had been operating as if justice had two sides and that he must continue to be an adversary to many of his brethren till the very day he leaves what he must have thought to have been the pinnacle of professional success.

44

His briefing on the police operations proceeded without the slightest trace of the zest with which he had greeted me earlier. Neither of our hearts was in it. I decided to break it off about a third through the agenda and went directly back to the guest house.

Those tragic eyes of the Senior Adjudicator would not let go of me. They kept imploring all the way.

"Please tell me it isn't so!"

45

I went straight into the kitchen, took out a glass and a bottle of whiskey, slumped into the easy chair, and gulped down several refills in quick succession. Why did I have to come ten thousand miles to crush such a gentle soul? I remember pounding my fist on the side table as I fell asleep.

The next thing I knew the aide wakened me. He kept reminding me that we did not have much time to get ready for the official Regional Administration dinner.

After a quick cold shower, my head cleared up considerably. I felt so much better that I was looking forward to another one of those evenings for friendship . . . for wine . . . for the spirit. I got dressed hurriedly, and stepped sprightly into the car. And off we went.

46

The Thursday evening affair promised to be a festive occasion. All of the government officials had been invited, as well as the persons I had met so far in Saikung and those I was scheduled to meet the following day. We toasted each other with much warmth, exchanged delightful jokes, and enjoyed ourselves no end.

As I sat down at the right of the Senior Regional Administrator at the banquet table, he leaned over and relayed the information that the wife of the Senior Regional Adjudicator had just phoned him. She reported that her husband had come home unexpectedly about three this afternoon and went straight to bed. She did not know what was bothering him but had never seen him so depressed and weakened before. She suspected it to be a severe intestinal disorder of some kind. Possibly staph poisoning at lunch. She tried to call the doctor but he would not let her do it. She wanted to extend their regrets for not being able to join me tonight.

My heart sank, I bravely tried to act out my role as honored guest. I suppose I responded properly to the toasts, downed the thirty-one glasses of wine, and so on. But truthfully, I didn't remember a thing. All I could recall very vaguely was seeing the Chief of Internal Peace Officers at a nearby table directly facing me, sitting with his eyes glued to his plate in order to avoid mine.

47

It was ten before I got up on Friday morning. The aide said that he had called me several times, but each time I would answer only to fall right back to sleep. We skipped breakfast and hurried out to the Saikung Indoctrination Center. After the three-hour visit, including lunch with the residents, I understood the significance of the name of the place.

There is no real equivalent in Chianglai for what we call a prison, the main purpose of which, and more often than not the *only* purpose, being incarceration and retribution. The daily routine of the residents of the Center is a very busy one. There is a carefully formulated training regimen, especially in the vocations. The machine shop, for example, is one of the best equipped in the area. It manufactures precision components for the Saikung Armament Works. Many of the better machinists transfer directly to the Works after graduation from the Center. When there are idle lathes, due to a decline in the Center population, people on the outside are admitted as part of the class. At the time of my visit, the latter group made up about thirty per cent out of the total enrollment of seven hundred in the training courses. It was difficult for me to tell them apart; all of them wore the same clothes.

Many of the instructors are older people, about half being between sixty and seventy years of age. Most of the older instructors work part-time under the aegis of the Old Age Activities program. The Manager of the Center is very pleased with them. He finds them more effective on the whole actually than the younger ones. They seem to be more open with the residents and much more likely to gain their respect and confidence. Their very presence appears to convey an atmosphere of calm. And most important of all, they are better able to provide

a perspective about living itself, a worthwhileness about going on and doing better, a mutuality about caring about others and being cared by others.

48

The operations of the Indoctrination Center reflects the philosophy of sentencing
in Chianglai. The only kinds of penalties are probational assignments and con-
finement in indoctrination centers. No monetary fines are levied, since these are
considered as disproportionately penalizing the poor, especially the innocent
dependents. Nor is there a death penalty—such a possibility doesn't even cross
their mind. The sentences at the indoctrination centers vary between one and ten
years. The minimum of one year is set because no one can be taught much in the
clarification of his views and the modification of his behavior in less than a year.
The maximum of ten years is based on the premise that one will not learn much
beyond that. Besides, ten years out of a man's life is the most that one should rea-
sonably demand from someone else for any given purpose. An added dimension is
involved in the more serious cases. There is a specially formulated intensified
indoctrination. The program then revolves around a three-year resolution of the
roots of anxiety within the individual and a rejuvenation of meaningfulness in his
life. Experience has shown that only five years of the intensive indoctrination is
usually sufficient to rehabilitate the most hardened of residents.

Once the resident is on the mend, the visiting privileges of families and
friends are extended from an afternoon a week to a day and a half on weekends.
These visits take place in the park area where the families may enjoy separate or
group picnics. This is always a happy time, even for those without any visitors.
The latter would usually be invited to join one or more families during the course
of a very short time. Friendships begun this way, I was told, continue on a very
close basis long after they leave the Center. As long as the residents remain in the
Center, their former salaries, less expenses connected with their upkeep at the
Center, are continued to their respective dependents. The rationale for this, of
course, is that the dependents should not be penalized for the breadwinner's temporary failure. But the most striking thing to me was the fact that it is the responsibility of the Manager of the Indoctrination Center to train and place the
graduate of his Center into a job to which he will report for work after a month's
vacation in transition.

When I expressed surprise at such a pampering of criminals, the Manager expressed surprise at my surprise. "But do we not all of us fail at one time or another?" he looked at me with puzzled eyes. "And when we do, do we not hope some brother will help us recover? And is this not one of the main reasons for living together?"

49

Our last official call in Saikung was the Art Center. Contrary to my expectations, I found it to be one of the most alive of all the places I've seen so far in the metropolis. As we entered the main entrance, we saw a group in one corner vigorously motioning and arguing, their high doing pitched voices producing a strange fugue. Two persons were doing the same in another corner. In the center courtyard, a painter sat dreamily looking at a clump of narcissus for fully twenty minutes and was still transfixed when we took our eyes off him. One of the individuals in the group saw us standing there, turned, smiled, quickly came over, and introduced himself as the Senior Painter of the Center.

He then took us on a tour of the various studios. The students and artists were of all ages. About thirty were painting outdoors. Every once in a while one of them would walk over to another and begin some kind of a conversation. Before long, more would join the pair. Again more motioning of the hands and arms and more sing-song animation. I remarked how impressed I was with the aliveness of the place. "Oh, that?" the Senior Painter pointed to the discussion group.

"They are debating over the best way of portraying the meaning of events and the qualities of reality which can be portrayed through painting. I imagine the average person has to begin learning the techniques of art in this fashion. By talking. And trying. And verbalizing until he reaches the very limit of words and convinces himself that words are really very poor means for the purpose. Then he gradually learns to converse with his eyes and his brush. When his spirit speaks through them, then he becomes a talented painter, like the old man watching the narcissus in the courtyard. This is what we try to pass on here at the Art Center. On rare occasions, however, someone appears who has gone far beyond the realm of the brush and the eyes. He is the master of what the Chinese call *Ch'i*. How he is able to communicate what he does, we do not know. But that he does, we do feel. This we cannot teach. We can but do homage."

50

We finally wound up in the main gallery, where the masterpieces of the renowned Naniphan were hung.

I was strangely attracted to the animal paintings especially. At first look her animals resemble those of any other good painter—a perfect likeness and all that. But if you pause for a split moment and look again, you experience an unusual sensation. The animals seem to be speaking to you—in a language you seem to comprehend—as if someone had written what is being said in invisible ink which you can read with your eye of inner stillness. The animals appear to be saying something different with the passage of time—as if engaged in friendly conversation. But the most peculiar feeling of all was that they also appear to be talking to each other as well.

As I stood there in pleasant reverie, their voices grew increasingly audible. And everything I heard was good—so good. Suddenly I was brought back to earth by the bells of the Mission of Saint Francis across the street, pealing the Angelus and announcing that the closing hour for the Art Museum has come.

51

Thak was sitting on the grass at the main entrance of the Sonbang National Park when I showed up early Saturday morning. He had flown up from Terkung to join me for the weekend. Two horses had been readied for us packed with the necessary camping gear and food.

I had been told by the aide that the Snoring National Park is Thak's favorite hideout. He would come here frequently for contemplating the future of the country. He would go on packing trips alone for days during crucial periods of national planning, when there were strong disagreements among the national leaders over fundamental issues. Nobody knows what he does or where he goes while he's here. But invariably, he would return to Terkung with a proposal which was unanimously accepted. And equally invariably, every one would marvel at its commonsensical simplicity and wonder why somebody else had not thought about it before all the arguments and—this is the good-natured jest around National Headquarters—Thak's paid vacation.

"Be careful about hurting the small animals who run freely about their home grounds, G. H.," was Thak's only instruction, as we took off into the luxuriant growth.

52

His warning came none too soon as we reined our horses away from the well-traveled path into Nature's own. Frogs and pythons. Monkeys chattering in the trees, cuckoos responding with repeated whistlings. Rainbow and argus pheasants, orange and brown grouse. The giant hornbill and the painted stork, babblers and drongos. Trout and mahseer jumping in every stream. Deep green *Myrtaceae* overhead, springy moss underfoot.

We broke into a clearing at the other edge of which was a herd of elephants lumbering along—two hundred of them. We heeded in another direction in order not to disturb them. As we rode along we came across two-horned rhinoceroses, tapirs, the bison-like gaur, the small ox-like banteng, several families of orangutans, hundreds of graceful gibbons swinging in the treetops, and thousands of small barking deers. At each encounter, Thak would create the least disturbance—like a grateful guest. Along the way, he would point out scores of fascinating details about Nature: a mother monkey teaching her young one how to peel a mango, the stronger mouse letting the weaker ones eat before him, the more effusive and more joyful singing of birds during their mating off-seasons when there are no ulterior motives attached, ants carrying bits of leaves to shield the mealy bug from the warm sun, slime molds exhibiting both animal and plant characteristics, and so on.

As I gazed at the towering 16,000-foot peaks caressed by the billowy clouds, at the endless canopy of green, at the teeming animals beneath, and then looked at ourselves—two mere echoes in the vibrant vitality of Nature—I began to appreciate for the first time of my life those sweeping Oriental landscapes with inconspicuous human figures in a way that I can only describe as "transcendent."

53

As we sat around the campfire after supper, I referred to the sensation which had come over me. How I have come to find a deeper significance in the landscapes by the Laian artists. How it is that here I felt so—the only word I could grope for was "free"—yes, free. Perhaps I feel so free because everything else around is free. The grass is not mowed but free to grow the way it naturally does. The shrubbery is not trimmed, but free to wave in the breeze the way it naturally does. The birds are not caged . . . at that word, I thought of our zoos. "Nobody had said anything about zoos, Thak," I picked up a new line of thought. "Where is the prettiest zoo in Chianglai?"

"There are no zoos in Chianglai," he announced matter-of-factly. It is against the Citizens' Prescriptions. "As you have just said, G. H., you feel so free. Why? Because everything else is free. Not only other human beings but other living beings as well. The meaning of this statement carries even more weight for us Laians because we consider the plants and animals to be our kin in Nature. How can we feel free if our brethren are imprisoned? That is why there are only game preserves and wildlife sanctuaries in Chianglai. No zoos. Only freedom."

"But don't you think that the zoo in Paris, for example, is quite educational for the French children? And besides, it certainly is one of the least innocuous forms of entertainment," I put forth the usual defense. "In our way of thinking, G. H." Thak met my justification head on, "we do not place our entertainment or even our education above our brother's freedom. That's why again I say: No zoos. Only freedom."

54

When I opened my sleepy eyes on Sunday morning, Thak was sitting against a tree with his elbows on his raised knees and his chin resting on his clasped hands. He was intently watching something.

At breakfast I asked what caught his fancy so. It was a field mouse giving birth to a litter. He was wondering how things went so smoothly without an obstetrician. To whom could the mother mouse have appealed for help had something gone wrong? Perhaps there is a God who watched over her. Perhaps the mouse did pray to God. But she did not do so in the way ministers say God should be approached. Perhaps God does not require his creatures to beg before he extends a hand. Why should God assist only the articulate? Only those aggressive in the asking? Only the sycophants continually smothering Him with praises? Only the ones with the proper credentials? Only the ones with intermediaries or spokesmen? No, the beneficence of the good God extends to all without the asking—just because He is good. "It is the same with government," Thak mused aloud. "The beneficence of the good government extends to all—the retiring as well as the militant, the unknown as well as the renowned, the distant as well as the nearby—just because it is good. The rest is mere words—excuses for the timid, camouflage for the cunning, license for the selfish."

Neither of us said very much all day as we dissolved into the surroundings. To be part of this majestic beauty was such a filling experience that somehow there must have been little room for words.

More National Enterprises

MAIKUNG

55

Thak went back to Terkung Sunday night as my aide and I flew on to take in more national enterprises and services at Maikung. Maikung was the first of the completely planned metropolises in Chianglai. Its population of 365,000 is approaching the programmed equilibrium.

There is no government edict restricting people as to the places where they may live. But the kinds of industries and opportunities for employment are carefully controlled. No heavy industries requiring a large labor pool are being planned for Maikung. The town is to be primarily a research and agricultural center capable of sustaining a population of about 400,000 rather comfortably. Available employment elsewhere is made known widely and offered to the interested parties. All expenses for interviews, retraining, and movement of household goods and family are covered by the Regional Administration.

Through such inducements the government has been able to keep the populations of its metropolises within fifteen per cent of the projected figures.

56

The Maikung Research Institute was our first stop on Monday morning. I have never come across an organizational structure of this kind before.

The Institute is divided generally—nothing seems to be rigid in the place, everything is *generally* so—into a group of individuals primarily versed in aspects of personal well-being and a second group primarily in aspects of social well-being, the latter including ecology and heritage. Aside from this loosely defined division, there are no others. The individuals somehow manage to join together into different teams varying in composition from time to time as the nature of their concerns change. At one of their frequent sessions, certain members of the team may suggest that their contributions are approaching diminishing returns and accordingly plan to bow out. Unless someone else could suggest a reason otherwise, they would leave the team for another, which has been seeking their assistance.

The Director of the Institute does not manage the activities in the conventional sense. He tries to maintain the general atmosphere and style of the place, invites capable men to join his staff so that there is a balanced representation of the essential skills, and ensures that the members do not become inbred in ideas. The individuals themselves shape the problems to be investigated, assemble the cadre, select the chairman *pro tempore*, obtain the results, and see to it that they are put into good use or at least passed on to the right place for further development. The system has been in effect for fifteen years. It has worked apparently to the satisfaction of everyone so far.

57

There are no written guidelines as to how these teams should be organized and who is authorized to start or stop anything. Somehow something gets going. Some of the projects are completed successfully and put into practice. Others meet with unsolvable complications and are abandoned.

After listening in on the discussions among four teams, ranging in size between two and seventy members, I gathered that they all began from the same basic point of reference. From that point of departure, a person or a small group would see whether they can come up with a new fundamental improvement over the initial situation. As the challenge extends beyond the limits of their competence, others would be invited to collaborate. Soon a full-blown project would be in being.

The common point of departure seems to be the change-to-value transform. How can the total well-being of the Laians as a people and the Laian as a person be improved in a harmonious fashion? Operationally, how can intellectual progress and natural transformations be assimilated into Laian values and Laian values be expressed through man-induced changes?

58

I expressed doubt about the kind of progress that can be expected in the sciences under such an approach to basic research. "How can they thrive if they are enmeshed in broad sociological issues?"

The Director did not disagree with the feeling that the chemist in the Institute should continue to perform chemistry like any competent chemist elsewhere. However, the philosophical context of what he does is very important in the Director's mind. If the chemist begins with the traditional Laian point of departure—and there is nothing to say that he must do so in the Institute—then his work will have a greater chance of a deeper trans-scientific significance even to himself, because it would bind him to his brethren's aspirations as well as his own as a chemist. This inspiration is different from that emerging as a response to a purely intellectual challenge leaving social consequences to reveal themselves as they will. After first discussing the general ramifications of pressing social needs and future possibilities with one or two others, say an ecologist or a psychologist in emphasis, the chemist can then quickly proceed with one or more associates into what would normally be regarded as pure chemistry. When his chemical results are obtained under the Laian approach, however, he had already established a bridge to social good. He can get together with the non-chemical members of the team and pass his findings on to the appropriate associate to use in accordance with the original framework of potentialities.

"This may sound good for the political purposes of Chianglai," I surmised. "But wouldn't this be bad for chemistry in the long run?" The Director did not think that it necessarily would. "The immense scientific talents of your great country and many others in the rest of the world are conducting experiments in chemistry in the way you recommend and will continue to do so. When added to that vast reservoir of science, the handful of scientists in Chianglai will hardly make a ripple I am afraid. Yet, even with our meager few, it may still be possible for us to call attention to the possibility that basic scientific research can be made intentionally and *a priori* relevant to human goodness and be guided by it. At least it can be made more so than has been the case in the past. This viewpoint may be our modest contribution to the place of science in the world of human affairs."

59

The agricultural complex is the largest in the country. Maikung's 75-degree temperature, 80 inches of rainfall annually, and rich alluvial black soil offer excellent growing conditions for rice. The fields stretch as far as one can see and the central plains of the region produce three fifths of the country's crop.

I was puzzled with the strange pattern of the paddies, which I observed from the plane yesterday. It did not follow typical agricultural practices. It did not even abide by sound principles of contour farming. It looked as if somebody had cut a pile of little cardboard pieces of odd shapes, tossed them over a large map on the floor, and ordered: "That's how the field will be laid out." When I checked into the matter, nobody was able to give a sensible rationale.

"Terkung directed it this way," someone finally divulged the secret. "But there was no reason given in the letter of instruction."

60

Because I had written a book on food preservation, a subject of some importance to Chianglai, the Director of the Agricultural Experiment Station invited me to deliver an impromptu lecture on the latest advances in the United States, after we finished our several cups of tea. I consented to do so.

The hastily convened conference began at ten thirty in the morning with an audience of about two hundred. For an hour, I discussed the accelerated methods of salting and pickling; low-cost refrigeration devices; non-toxic fumigation of grains and cereals; efficient dehydration of vegetables; freeze dehydration of meats; sterilization by atomic radiation; temperature, sunlight, and oxygen effects on the browning reaction, fat rancidity, and other deteriorate changes in the stored food itself; and the latest plastic films and packaging materials and techniques. Questions were submitted in writing as the talk progressed. After the lecture, I began to answer them one slip of paper after another from the pile on the table. At three thirty in the afternoon—with no break of any kind in-between—there were still about a hundred more on the pile and more kept dribbling in. The Director decided to bring the session to a close and thanked me profusely. The audience expressed its appreciation with a long applause. I barely made the men's room in time.

61

My aide and I relaxed before dinner meandering around the rice fields. We zig-zagged along the raised pathways disturbing the ubiquitous paddy birds as we went along. The southwest monsoon rain had recently begun and the soil was wet enough to be worked. In two months the ditches and irrigation canals will be filled with water. Now it is plowing time. The water buffaloes were being ridden home by the little boys astride their backs forming tranquilly moving silhouettes against the horizon at sunset. One of them with a lad playing a flute came in the opposite direction and waited at the junction so that we could pass.

As we met, I gingerly patted the water buffalo on the forehead and smiled at the lad. He smiled back. "What's his name?" "Good Brother." "Who gave him the name of Good Brother?" "I did." "And why did you call him Good Brother?" "He helps us with our hard work. He never steps on our brethren's rice. He never hurts anybody. That is why I call him Good Brother." "What was the song you were playing? It sounded so pretty." "The tiger song."

His face lit up and he burst into a delightful tune:

Brother tiger, brother tiger
Oh please, do lower your roar.
Did you not promise, dear brother
You'll ne'er be angry any more?

Our good brother, the buffalo,
Will help us with our rice this spring.
When you roar, his horns dip low.
How can he then do his plowing?

62

The Manager of the Maikung Regional Farm hosted the evening picnic. The main attraction was a special barbecue.

Five hours were spent preparing it. A long trench, two feet by two feet, was dug. Dried yang wood was laid on the bottom with a layer of rocks on top and yet another of wood. The top layer of wood was lit. As it was reduced to coals and the bottom layer began to flame slowly, quarters of pork were placed on a rack about four inches above the hot coals. A semi-cylindrical cover of corrugated tin with open ends was placed with the sides on the ground and the tin itself just about half an inch from the pork surface. The quarters were turned over every fifteen minutes and basted. The sauce was *nuoc yeou*, with some *mei jiu*, Tabasco, paprika, chopped garlic, chopped ginger, salt, sugar, and spiced bean paste.

Positively delicious. I've never tasted such a dish before nor since. What kind of flavor? You might imagine a blend of Texas Barbecue, Chinese roast pork, and Hawaiian *kailua* pig—with a dash of *Grand Marnier*.

63

We devoted Tuesday morning to the two agencies located here at Maikung but working directly out of the Headquarters of the Saikung Regional Administration. These were the Metropolis and the Ecology Agencies.

Being a manager of a metropolis in Chianglai appears much more stressful than being the Mayor of Chicago. There is no political unit recognized as a metropolis. The Metropolis is merely a geographical term, like a valley. It may be looked upon as a valley of men. It is a location where the population density of the contiguous communities is so high, that a large degree of common services and standardization among them is required for economic reasons. The Manager of the Metropolis is first and foremost a coordinator, an ameliorator, and an arbiter. A metropolis of a million generally involves some twenty-five independent communities. The Manager exerts no line authority over the communities and relies primarily on persuasion. When a community is obviously out of line, however, the Manager can appeal to the Metropolis Agency. The Regional Headquarters can then hand down a ruling to the stubborn community. Such an inference of unwillingness to cooperate for the good of the greater mass causes considerable loss of face and community leaders do not wish to risk such a possibility except for very grave issues. Because of this leverage the Manager of the Metropolis is usually able to implement any reasonable scheme, almost never, however, without considerable convincing, cajoling, and compromising.

What the Director of Medical Welfare Service told me at the picnic last night now appears quite understandable. He said that of all the different occupations in Chianglai, the managers of metropolises have the highest incidence of heart attacks.

64

The Director of the Metropolis Agency doubts that the average metropolis can provide the good life for most of its residents if the population exceeds much over 500,000. The good life *can* be attained with Herculean effort if the metropolis of up to a million is situated all by itself surrounded by large reaches of land. Then the residents would at least be able to commune with living Nature other than themselves once in a while and reinvigorate their fundamental belonging, so to speak. But he has no hope for urban centers above the two and a half million mark, no matter what is attempted. Life for the residents of such agglomerations can only mean varying degrees of dissatisfactions.

He acknowledged that national interests do require a certain number of large metropolises for industrial reasons. But a high price has to be paid and the nation should take extraordinary measures to soften the stresses of urban living. "When does an atomic bomb explode?" he expounded on the theme. "I'm told when the packing density of neutrons exceed a critical mass. The same principle should hold with the packing density of human beings." Their calculations on the theoretical frequencies of contact among people as a function of the mean free path between individuals, the velocity of travel and communication, and the drive of exploitive intentions have led him to the figure of 500,000.

"That limit, however, applies to a population of quite a high moral character—one that is slightly above that of the Laians at the moment," he stressed what appeared to him as a most important qualification. "Otherwise a population of only two may be explosive!"

65

The Director of the Metropolis Agency was such an interesting person with an analytical approach to things that is not usual among the Laians that I overstayed my time. This left only a half-hour courtesy call on the Director of the Ecology Agency, our last stop in Maikung.

A standout feature of the concept of ecology as held by the people of that Agency is the complete acceptance of changing the flora and fauna of our planet. Pollution, of course, should be controlled. This goes without saying. But unlike the environmental protectionists elsewhere, it is considered unnatural to attempt to freeze the ecological balance in its present state. This cannot be done in any case. Evolution and change should be welcomed, including the extinction of species, if, and this is a big *if*, that change is consonant with the overall harmony of Nature. Accordingly, the Agency focuses its concerns on influencing the many concomitant changes so that they form a harmony for all the brethren—men, animals, and plants.

The Director was disappointed that I was not able to stay longer. "I had hoped that you would have had more time with us. We would have liked to exchange views on the basic atmosphere which we are attempting to cultivate in our agency. It is the metaphysical search for harmony and its practical expression in the living world. It is a very subtle and difficult synthesis. I was personally looking forward to having the benefit of your learned advice on this important matter. Please do us the honor of visiting again."

66

We sped toward the airport so that our little plane could make the next leg of our journey before sundown. The aide motioned the driver to press on the gas. He did. A mongoose darted across the road. The driver stepped on the brakes. Too late. The front and rear wheels went right over the poor creature.

The driver got out of the car. Looking back at the still and bloody mass that once was a highly intelligent living being, he stood motionless with a few very soft sobs. The aide started to tell him to get back in and drive on. But I held his arm. He got the signal and we both sat back, letting the man resume when he felt ready.

Instead of doing so right away, the driver walked in the opposite direction toward a nearby shack. He spoke to the man sitting on the doorstep, who disappeared for a moment and came back with a shovel. The driver slowly looked about and chose a spot under the shade of a spreading Banyan tree. He dug a hole, four feet deep, and carefully squared the sides and leveled the bottom. Breaking off four fronds from a nearby banana clump, he neatly wrapped the limp form and gently lowered the body into the grave. After meticulously straightening out a twisted frond, he shoveled in the soil. He then stood beside the mound for a full minute with his head bowed. Finally he returned the shovel with a silent nod of gratitude, sat behind the wheel, and drove off—without ever looking us in the eye again.

Eastern Sector Military Command

PNOMKUNG

67

On our approach to the Pnomkung military airport, we saw a regiment of troops standing there. The pilot leaned over and told us that orders had just come from Terkung to render me full military honors. The General stepped forward as our plane came to a full stop, snapped a salute, and introduced himself as Colonel-General Koasadwin, Commanding General of the Eastern Sector Military Command. He welcomed me in the name of the National Commander of Defense and invited me onto the reviewing stand.

The troops were ordered to attention. The national anthem was played. The General then escorted me on an inspection around the front and back. I was struck by the unevenness. About half of the regiment looked quite military. The other half was rather spotty, especially the last platoon. I complimented the General, nonetheless, for his fine outfit and he seemed genuinely pleased. The soldiers then trooped in review. The band played a martial piece with the air of a Scottish fantasy. The first battalion goose-stepped in perfect cadence as it passed our reviewing stand. The second battalion shuffled along in waves. The third was awful. When the last platoon did an "eyes right," a soldier in the front row center hit his cheek against the rifle, which dropped out of his hand, tripped up three soldiers to his right, who went lurching onto the ground. More flying rifles, cascading into no less than ten sprawling bodies.

I had a hard time containing myself from bursting into a fit of laughter. I looked straight ahead as if nothing out of the ordinary had happened. The General did the same.

68

"Because of the temperament of our people and the poverty of our economy, our military strategy cannot be anything else but defensive in character," the General introduced the Wednesday's morning's briefing. "Internally, you will find the economy, land usage, and routines of life geared to a protracted resistance to invaders. Externally, our forces are designed for sustained spoiling combat ten miles beyond our northern border just over the Sonbang Mountain Range, forty miles beyond our eastern border just over the Baobang Mountain Range, and two hundred and fifty miles out to sea to the west and south, just beyond our normal fishing grounds.

"I myself am responsible for the Eastern Sector. My counterpart is responsible for the western half. Both of us report to the National Commander of Defense in Terkung, who in turn reports to the National Administrator for Foreign Affairs.

"Since you will not have an opportunity to visit other military installations, I have been directed by the National Commander of Defense to present the total picture of our defense posture. Our presentation will cover five areas: First, our organization and mission. Second, future planning. Third, our basic military strategy. Fourth, paramilitary defense. Fifth, a tour of our arsenal to see the latest land and air equipment, with a movie of sea equipment. My staff is here to provide any desired details. Do you have any questions at this point, sir? No? Lieutenant, proceed."

69

"As General Koasadwin has outlined, the country is divided into two sectors, the Eastern and the Western," the lieutenant sharply pointed to the respective areas on the wall map. "As Commanding General of the Eastern Sector, General Koasadwin is responsible for complete military activities in the region from the Sonbang Mountain Range to the north, the Luangkong River to the east, the Wakong River to the west, and two hundred miles out to sea, including the capital of our country, Terkung." More stabbings at the map. And so went half an hour of orientation with a succession of organization charts, mission statements, and statistical graphs.

Each sector is divided into three land combat corps area and one sea area. The air combat corps covers both land and sea. Logistic centers operated by the Regional Administrators provide material, repair, maintenance, and research and engineering. A Military Futurity Agency is a tenant in the Eastern Sector and operates under the direct command of the National Commander of Defense. This Agency is responsible for evolving future strategies and tactical concepts, analyzing intelligence data for military implications, formulating the required military specifications for future material, adapting advances in foreign military doctrines and material to Laian forces, studying the augmentation of defensive capabilities by modifications in the civilian sectors, and integrating military strategy with that of foreign relations.

"We do not view the military forces *per se* as the ultimate line of defense," the General interjected his thought. "The ultimate deterrent is the will of the people to defend their way of life, their land, their memories, their posterity's future. That is why we in the military side of the house give considerable attention to our impact upon the civilian side. If what we do weakens the other side, then our actions become self-defeating."

70

The Operations Officer then discussed their military strategic outlook. An attack from the north is not anticipated because of the impenetrable mountains. The chances of an invasion from the east are higher, but still relatively low. The next door neighbor is only a third the size of Chianglai and the people come from the same philosophical nonaggressive culture. But the country on the other side had been aggressive throughout its history. Its cyclical behavior involves a period of about sixty years. The characteristic phases are: licking war wounds, undergoing guilt-feelings and over-compensating acts of charity, yearning for more living room and rice-producing lands to take care of her expanding population, weakening her intended victim by subtle means, provoking a border incident, followed immediately with open warfare. For the last thirty years, it has been steadily infiltrating the next door neighbor with cultural and commercial influences. Having begun the erosion of the native religion and moral standards, it is now working toward an economic and financial domination. Some incident about protecting nationals and investments can be stirred up by the aggressive country at any time she cares to at this junction of time. Chianglai is ready for such a contingency. But since a military assistance pact exists between the next door neighbor and Chianglai, it is doubtful that the other country, which is about equal militarily to Chianglai but without any reliable allies, would like to start trouble in the foreseeable future.

There is a far greater likelihood of attack from the sea. The 950-mile coastline is dotted with fine landing sites, so many in fact that it would be difficult to station fixed defenses all along the western and southern sea frontier in the light of the limited military budget. Available intelligence suggests that Country X is eying this region of the globe, particularly the neighbor to the east. Since Country X is aware of the existing military assistance pact, she is probably preparing to take on both countries together. Analysis of her past strategies of conquests and of the psychological indicators gleaned from the current remarks of her middle line officers suggests that an initial salient at the southern port of Haikung on the delta of the Wakong River may well be the case, followed by a push inland about twenty miles then a swing northeastward to cut off the neighbor's main petroleum pipeline into the interior and her rice basin.

Based on this estimate of the world situation, Chianglai has given its naval forces the largest share of the budget, followed by the air force. These two arms will have to repel the enemy far out at sea to prevent the landing of their armies. "Should the superior army of Country X reach land, however, we shall have to fall back eventually on a long war," the Colonel stipulated. "Our tactics on land will rely primarily on mobile units of battalion size, a score or so of regimental combat teams, and civilian guerillas. During this phase the strength of character of the people, as General Koasadwin has just reiterated, will be decisive."

71

The Colonel next took up the manner in which the country has been organized so that it can survive against a superior military power. "From your visits to the various places so far, you have undoubtedly noticed what might have appeared to be an inefficient layout of farm lands, unnecessary duplication of effort among communities, and other apparent signs of poor management. Undoubtedly many of them are indeed signs of actual needs for improvement. But most of them have been intentionally set up that way for paramilitary defense. Our rice paddies, for example, make excellent tank traps. They are therefore laid out in such a fashion as to preclude a broad armor blitz across our country. We can handle the single columns of scattered tanks with mines and hand-held heat-seeking missiles with much greater promise of success."

The communities and the metropolises are also arranged with military that the enemy forces considerations in mind. Chianglai's strategy is premised on the assumption that the enemy forces will employ nuclear weapons up to a hundred kiloton yield, while her own will be without any nuclear arms. Accordingly, the size of Chianglai's metropolises is controlled in order that no single direct hit by a nuclear warhead or three near-misses will wipe out more than two per cent of the population and that no large scale nuclear effort will destroy more than thirty. The national twenty-year plan currently calls for only two metropolises between half and one million, six between 100,000 and 500,000, twenty between 50,000 and 100,000, and the rest below 50,000. In addition, the largest single metropolis will be limited to 2.5 million. In the future, no cities more than 300,000 in size will be established within fifty miles of each other.

In order to carry on sustained guerrilla resistance, the communities are to be biologically self-sufficient, at least in cooperation with their immediate neighbors. In this way, given basic arms caches locally and larger well distributed depots inland, backed up by multiple routes and sources of re-supply, Chianglai should be able to hold out for quite some years in protracted exasperational warfare.

72

At supper in the General's quarters, our conversation centered around the servicemen themselves.

The main strength of the defense forces rests in a cadre of about 75,000 men. These are the professionals. About half of them serve through at least two generations of military men originally from tribal stock in the northeastern foothills of the Sonbang and the large island off the southern coast. Fine, tough, and disciplined. The rest of the national force of 227,000 men are—in the General's own words—"not worth a damn, sir."

"The chief problem," the General gave vent to his frustrations, "is teaching them how to kill. They just don't want to. Instinctively and deeply ingrained, I suppose. I know that our national personality is one of gentleness and compassion for our fellow men. But you can't win wars—even defensive ones—by being gentle and compassionate, as you from the militarily powerful nations so well know."

73

Thursday was spent at the Armory. It housed the usual assemblage of military matériel, including land mines of quite modern design, personnel carriers, a few light tanks and planes of 1955 vintage. The clothing was identical to those worn by laborers, except for a few insignias. Rations consist of rice, salt fish, and dried sausages of the same variety that I had for lunch with the Prakung farmers.

The General showed particular pride in the small arms. The rifles, machine guns, recoilles weapons, and the mortar have been invented by the Military Futurity Agency and produced in Chianglai. They are adapted for local use to the last detail. The mortar base plate, for example, is a cleverly fitted arrangement of three pieces of light metal-plastic composite, each of which can be hand-carried by a small man over long distances. The weapons nestle into each other for maximum packing density in caches. The moving parts are much simplified for easy field maintenance.

When I inquired about the picture on the wall of what seems to be one of the latest models of jet fighters, the General snorted: "Humpff! Got a squadron of them *free* several years ago through military aid from some ally. Since then, they have been using all of the loose cash I have in the entire Eastern Sector. War is getting too damned expensive."

74

The movie of naval operations and equipment was more impressive. No doubt about it. The Navy gets the best. Nothing big like a cruiser. But solid stuff, well tailored to their mission and strategy. A few small missile frigates, a score of what seems to be a cross between a missile frigate and a destroyer, destroyers, and assorted crafts.

The backbone of the fleet is a submersible ship, designed by the Military Futurity Agency and produced in five different plants in Chianglai. I estimate the present output at about three a month. It carries a machine gun on the starboard and port deck, a protected position for hand-held weapons fore and aft, and four torpedoes, which can be fired while submerged. It is highly resistant to depth charges through a special barrier of active concussion absorption. It is able to replenish its supplies from secret mobile underwater supply points. Normal complement of ten men. Can be out for twenty days without resupply with a cruising range of 500 miles. One of the standard defensive tactics involves lying on the sandy bottoms in different formations so that it would be practically impossible for an enemy ship to approach shore without coming within range of three of these torpedo launchers.

Another ingenious defensive system is a fast moving gunboat equipped with a missile, the guidance system of which is locked to the ship's centroid. The missile flies above five feet above the water surface, pulling an underwater hydrodynamically shaped mine. When launched at night it is impossible to counter. During the day, as the weaponeers would put it: the probability of hit is .94; the probability of kill is .89.

The Capital Revisited

TERKUNG

75

Thak met us at the airport upon our return to the capital on Friday morning. He suggested a leisurely stroll for the day. Strolling is much more conducive for searching deliberations, he said, than sitting around a conference table in some stuffy office. The chauffeur dropped us off in the middle of town and the aide took our bags to the boat for the overnight cruise down the Wakong River to Haikung.

We wended our way through the jovial lanes of Laians. Somehow I felt good looking at their faces. Their ranks thinned out as we moved out of the central district. We then walked along the dirt paths in one of the thickly vegetated parks that are distributed throughout the metropolis.

Of a sudden, I found myself lurching forward, as if I had accidentally tripped over something. Looking back I found nothing over which I could have stumbled—nothing except possibly a tiny centipede. My foot must have refused to step on it.

76

As we wandered along Thak answered a host of questions I had jotted down during my trip. He was extremely patient. My eyes must have expressed disbelief at just about every other reply or so. In each case he would deliberately backtrack and describe the fundamental values of good living as the Laians *see* them, how these considerations call for certain kinds of attitudes, how these attitudes are translated into general policies as well as specific practices, and how the method of implementation to achieve those purposes without jeopardizing other fundamental values calls for just the particular reply over which I had shown some skepticism.

After he had resolved all of the questions I had on my mind, at least to the point of my understanding of the underlying reasons from his standpoint, he turned to me for any advice on beneficent government that *I* might be able to give him, based on my observations in Chianglai and on my own knowledge and experience in government in general. "I may be able to provide a little suggestion here and there on the operational details in a few specialties that I happen to be expert in," I evinced a degree of modesty which I later recalled as not at all characteristic of myself. "But as far as the fundamental approach to making our brethren in Chianglai happy is concerned, my experience here has made me very humble. When I accepted your invitation to visit Chianglai, Thak, I thought I would be able to bring you some good ideas. Now, I don't think I can offer anything of value . . . not a thing."

I thought for a minute and continued. "As a matter of fact, I had discussed the situation with a brilliant and close friend of mine, Dr. Schwartz, who is senior partner of that very well-known American management consulting firm, McKenzie Associates. We spent five weekends drawing up a basic framework for Chianglai's future evolution. I brought along a copy of the plan, four other reports that I had prepared myself, and two books just off the press by our most respected public administrators in the United States. I had intended to give them to you at this time. But I tore them up into little pieces and threw them away . . . when I got back to the guest house . . . after the official banquet . . . in Saikung."

77

Thak hailed one of the noodle vendors and we sat on the grass for lunch. He exchanged a few pleasantries in Laiese with the man who stood nearby and, before long, they were engaged in a serious dialogue. From the looks of things, it almost appeared as if the pupil Thak was sitting at the feet of his master. We handed our empty bowls and chopsticks back to the vendor, wished him well, and went on our way. I commented that the conversation must have been most interesting. "And most instructive to me," Thak added.

He had talked to the vendor about his lot, his wife, the family, what the future had in store for him, and so on. Thak confessed that he was deeply impressed by the fellow and that he was somewhat taken aback with a kind of guilt-feeling when the vendor described some of the things he would do if *he* were running the government. Particularly pointed were his remarks on the neglect of the government for the private family enterprises. He felt that the government was correct in keeping the basic wealth of the country in the hands of the people and in not letting individuals control large parts of it to exploit others. He also appreciated the importance of the national enterprises and the community cooperatives as the economic backbone of the nation. But he could see no office in the government to whom he, as a small family entrepreneur, can go for advice and help. To him, this meant that the government was hoping that his kind would soon disappear through inattention. "If that happens," the man said, shaking his finger at Thak, "it will be a sad day for Chianglai." It will mean that Chianglai has lost its sense of reasonableness. And without reasonableness, the society reverts to savagery. "Is this desire of the little entrepreneur not a reasonable one?" the man pleaded. "Do I not bring worthwhile and timely service, and I hope some pleasure, to you and your honorable brother now as I serve you the best that our humble kitchen can offer? Our profit is not excessive—only half again as much as the skilled worker in the national factories. But my wife and I work much longer hours. We do not take advantage of others. Why does the government want to eliminate such reasonable brethren?" The vendor called attention to the fact that there are other family enterprises that are making much more valuable contributions to the Laian society than his. The wood carver next door to him, for example, came from a long line of wood carvers. Being a Cantonese, the noodle vendor could not claim the wood carver's kind of deep intimacy with Chianglai himself, and besides his skill is not the kind that families take pride in handing from father to son. "But when I pass the wood carver's little shop every morning," the vendor's eyes lit up with vicarious pride, "I say to myself: *There* is Chianglai . . . roots ten thousand years long." Then his eyes turned sad and disappointed. "The government should understand this. There is no government official who can point to his office and say the same thing. This is the main reason why I feel so depressed over the government's negligence of the small businessman. I came to Chianglai when I was twelve years old. I have come to love my brethren here. I am afraid for them. Because when the roots are destroyed, the bright flowers above the ground will soon wilt, and the plant will be dead forever." That was the gist of what transpired between Thak and the noodle vendor.

Thak withdrew into another one of his meditative silences, which I had learned to respect back in the days of Montparnasse. He sat motionless for fully five minutes, dreamily looking, it seems, into the far distance in space and time. Then he took a pen and pad out of his coat pocket and jotted down a few notes. After that, he was his charming outward self again and we resumed our stroll.

78

On the way to the docks, I found myself in an unsettled state of mind. A very important piece of this philosophical and political jigsaw puzzle seemed to be missing. I felt apprehensive over the future of these people, of whom I have become so much a part during the past three weeks. Encouraged by Thak, I finally spoke up. As I did, my fears became clearer. There is no written Constitution to preserve their rights. No overall religious leader to bring them the word and love of God. Not even a Trans-Socialist Party to guide their secular destiny. What insurance is there against an oppressive dictatorship being imposed in the future by some clique? I began to feel sorry for my Laian brethren. I could almost see that dreadful day at hand.

"Where does beneficence come from?" Thak asked rhetorically. "Surely not in something written or in something said. And can beneficence find its origin *only* at a certain date in the historical eons? At the hour a Constitution was formulated? Or the day a particular church was founded? Surely not so. And does beneficence *only* flow in one direction? From the top to the bottom? Surely not so. And is beneficence to be exercised *only* among men? So that animals can be hurt or shrubs trampled or Nature defiled? Surely not so. Totalitarian oppression, democratic oppression, religious oppression, economic oppression—these are but a few of the many disruptions of the good life. There are others. Mania of power, vanity of wealth, conceit of the intellect, arrogance of the soul, fraud of fame . . . these are even more disastrous to a satisfying life."

Thak hesitated for a few seconds and then continued: "Remember the answer that Senior National Administrator Nam gave you at his home the second night after your arrival when you asked him about his main preoccupation? He said something to the effect that it was maintaining an indomitable faith, a stability of trust, a sinking of natural and deep anchorage into the heritage of the country. Something about the love of the land, the sky, the people . . . the mountains, the trees, the animals . . . the rivers and lakes, the streams and rivulets, the tiny pebbles and the little ferns. Well, *there* and *only* there lies the lasting assurance of the future. Where else?" As I stepped onto the gangplank, I thought I almost saw what he was driving at—but not quite.

79

Moon high above the mangrove forest and *Nipa* palms on the banks of the Wakong. Boat moving smoothly downstream with the tide. Thak and I leaning against the deck rail. Without a word. Looking out into that vast restfulness. So serene, so peaceful, so free. I caught myself—did I say *free*?

Can't understand how it can be. Can't understand why the people are so happy. Thak's forgotten words at the statue of Keikitran and Eleevan when we visited the Central National Park on my first weekend here came back to me: "If you can absorb the spirit behind that assemblage in bronze, you will grasp . . . what makes Chianglai tick."

"Thak," I broke the silence. "Who is Keikitran . . . and who is Eleevan?" So he related the Legend of Keikitran and Eleevan.

80

Keikitran was the favorite offspring of the God Akuatran. During his adolescence, the godling became restless over the ever present perfection in the Goddom of Akuatran. He would often sneak away to his own secret garden on the banks of a beautiful river in a tiny out of the way planet called Earth. He loved the way the animals and the birds would greet him, the way the flowers would smile at him, the way the trees would wave at him. Everything was so fresh and spontaneous. Keikitran used to remove little thorns and burrs from the animals feet and fur. He would freshen the wilting shrubs with water and feed the birds with berries in his hand. He began to learn many new things. Kindness, for one. He never knew what it meant before. There was no need to be kind in his father's heaven—everything was perfect; nobody needed any help. The feeling for a creature in need created a strong bond between him and the residents of that charming valley. Soon he came to know practically every animal and every plant by name. All the animals and plants, the waters and the winds, the earth and the sky were happy whenever Keikitran would come and visit. While Keikitran was lying by the side of an animal path one day, he heard an anxious chirping across the way. "Keiki! Keiki!" Some bird was calling for help. Keikitran jumped up and dashed into the shrubbery. And sure enough, there was a shivering kitten—all black except tipped with white at the chin and paws and with white splashes at the front of the neck, chest, and abdomen. A loose boulder had just fallen from the hillside, rolled down the path, and crushed his front right paw. It was a pitiful and gory sight. Keikitran did not know what to do—he had never seen suffering in heaven before. For the first time he knew what it was to be pained by someone else's pain. He learned the real meaning of brotherhood. His heart quickened. He did what best he knew. He sat by the kitten's side and stroked his forehead. He split open a dried gourd, filled it with milk from the goat, who stood by with the other animals and birds, and placed the dish before the kitten. But the kitten did not move. Sadness descended over the land. For three days and three nights, no one said anything. The winds were subdued. The sky was darkened. Early on the fourth morning, there was a feeble "meow." Everybody looked up and turned. There was the kitten with bright open eyes. He stretched his neck toward the milk. Keikitran moved it within reach. The kitten lapped it all up and purred loudly. Then he leaned back on his hind legs, lifted his injured paw, and slowly and gently began to lick it. The swelling was subsiding and the bluish color was turning into a healthy red. Suddenly the whole valley burst into song. The breeze blew blissfully again. The sun shone through. Keikitran was in tears. So overjoyed was he. After several more days, the kitten hobbled about on three legs. In two weeks he was fully himself again, except for the partial loss of a claw on the inner side of his right foot about an inch above the ground and an almost unnoticeable outward turn of the right paw. He was then given the name of Eleevan by the little bird.

Keikitran and Eleevan became close friends and Keikitran wanted to invite Eleevan to stay with him in heaven. But the Chancellor of the Book would have no part of it, for it was written in Rule 17: "Only the perfect shall enter the Goddom of Akuatran." Eleevan did not qualify because of the damaged claw and the out-turned paw. Keikitran appealed to his father. But it was of no use. Not even Akuatran himself could deviate from the Book. So perfect was it.

But Keikitran would not be separated from his friend. If Eleevan could not stay in Keikitran's place, then Keikitran would stay in Eleevan's. So in the year 1,022,623 B. C. Keikitran left the Goddom of Akuatran with his beautiful bride by the name of Eeonna. They settled in his secret garden in a place now known as Terkung and gave rise to the Laian people and the Tran Dynasty, which reigned in an unbroken line for over a million years.

A Reservation at Departure

HAIKUNG

81

"*Au revoir!*" Just as I was about to step into the plane, Thak called out again. "How about the answers, G. H.—the answers to the two questions I asked you after the first briefing? Yes or no?"

"To the first question," I shouted above the whine of the jet engines, "the answer is yes. To the second question . . . I don't know." We both smiled fondly and waved. A film of tears began to blur my vision of him. I turned sharply into the plane.

The door slammed shut. The plane taxied away and took off. I leaned back on the reclining chair, wiped my watery eyes, and reflected: Perhaps I should have said yes to the second question as well. . . . But such a heathen doctrine. . . . Even if I did feel favorably inclined during my weaker moments. . . . Even if I did wish them well. . . . How could I admit to it? I'm sure Thak understood. . . . Yet I'm not so sure. . . . Come to think of it, my last sight of him *was* blurred . . . blurred in my own eyes . . . by something within myself . . . over which I had no control. . . . I did meet him more than half way though. . . . It's the best I could do . . . for old time's sake.

APPENDIX

I. The Country of Chianglai

Population: 42,000,000

Ethnic Composition: Equilibrium race of about five eighths Oriental, an eighth Caucasian, an eighth Polynesian, an eighth Others.

Language: Laiese (Phonetic ideograph)

Religion: 55 per cent Pantheistic Hinayana Buddhists, 20 per cent Agnostics, 10 per cent Christians, 5 per cent Moslems, 10 per cent Others.

Geography: 225,000 square miles. Bounded on north by Sonbang Mountain Range, with peaks up to 16,700 feet, on east by Luangkong River, on west and south by the Laian Sea. Wakong River flows North-South bisecting the country longitudinally.

Climate: Tropical and subtropical.

Form of Government: Trans-Socialist.

Industry: Chiefly agricultural, including rice, tea, teak, yang, fish. Some coal, iron, uranium phosphate, tin, and tungsten mining. Small scale manufacturing, including tin and iron smelting, silk textiles, lacquer ware, porcelains, ceramic figures, hardwood arid ivory carving, weapons for internal use. Tourist trade discouraged.

National Sport: *Naloeen* (Flying swallow).

History: The earliest written record consists of crude pictorial ideographs carved on a tablet of worship to the god Eleevan. This was authenticated as having been fashioned in 625 B. C. At that time the country was pastoral with many little villages living peacefully together, sharing the same language and customs. There was a person called the Elder to whom the people would look up as a man of courage and wisdom, he exercised no official authority. But he was respected as a direct descendant of Keikitran, the legendary ancestor of the Laians. People would come to him for help in times of crises, he would adjudicate disagreements between villages. His suggestions were not binding on either party. There is no evidence, however, to indicate that his judgments have ever been disregarded.

A more formal system of government began about the seventh century A.D. Although the Elder became a full-time leader, the system was still very loose. Troops and taxes were purely voluntary—the different villages contributing whatever they felt they could afford, which varied considerably from time to time.

Signs of formality and efficiency became visible beginning about the sixteenth century when the younger rulers began to employ the Christian missionaries, who began to arrive in sizeable contingents as advisors. Compulsory taxation and a conscript army were instituted in 1710 when European tradesmen brought the ideas with them.

In 1763 two Dutch warships landed on the southern coast and after three short skirmishes of muskets against bows and arrows and two booming salvoes from the ships—something the Laians had never seen or heard before, the local authorities surrendered. Chianglai became a Dutch colony. Dutch money poured in and soon Chianglai became the major commercial center and rice producer in the region. In 1803 the French landed troops on the northwestern shores and occupied that quarter of the country. A three-way war developed among the French, the Dutch, and the native insurgents. The indecisive free-for-all lasted three years, when France and Holland decided to pool their resources and divide the spoils. The insurgents were liquidated within a year. The western half of Chianglai went to the French and the eastern half to the Dutch. Within less than two years, another war broke out over the control of taxes on local fishermen in the Wakong River. Fierce fighting took place all along the central border, see-sawing back and forth for two years until the French navy swept the Dutch off the southern sea and cut off the port of Haikung. Within a year the Dutch were brought to their knees. France ruled the entire country from 1845 to 1914. In 1914 France was forced to move her main body of troops back to Europe to fight in World War I. Overnight a local uprising occurred. After two years of fighting a peace treaty was concluded, restoring independence to the Kingdom of Chianglai. The country was overrun again in 1938 by the Japanese. The young son of the assassinated emperor was placed as puppet ruler over a Japanese dominated country. An underground of revolutionaries was organized supported by a worldwide network of Chianglai exiles and overseas students. World War II resulted in the expulsion of the Japanese. The reins of government were handed by the victorious Allies back to the relatives of the former puppet emperor. The underground burst out in widespread action. After two years, the revolutionaries succeeded in over-throwing the kingdom and peace was established in 1947.

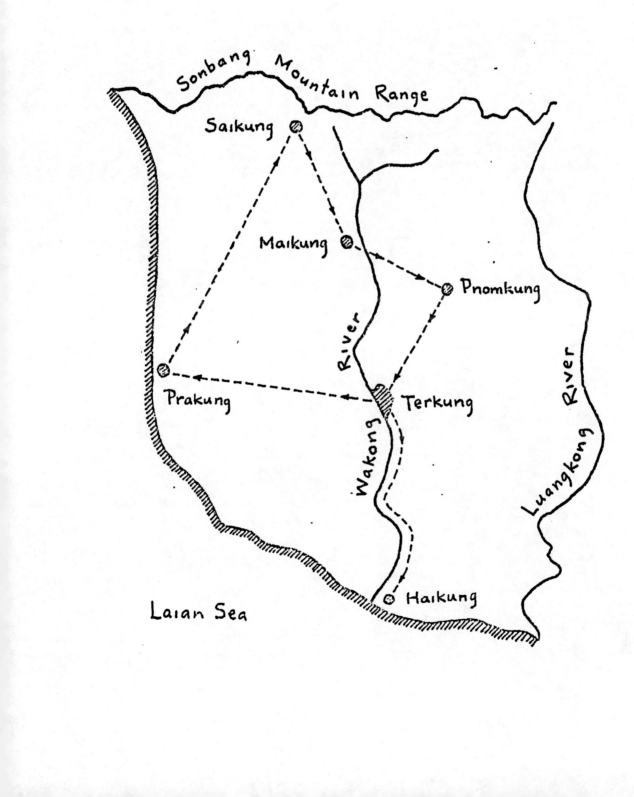

GOVERNMENT OF CHIANGLAI

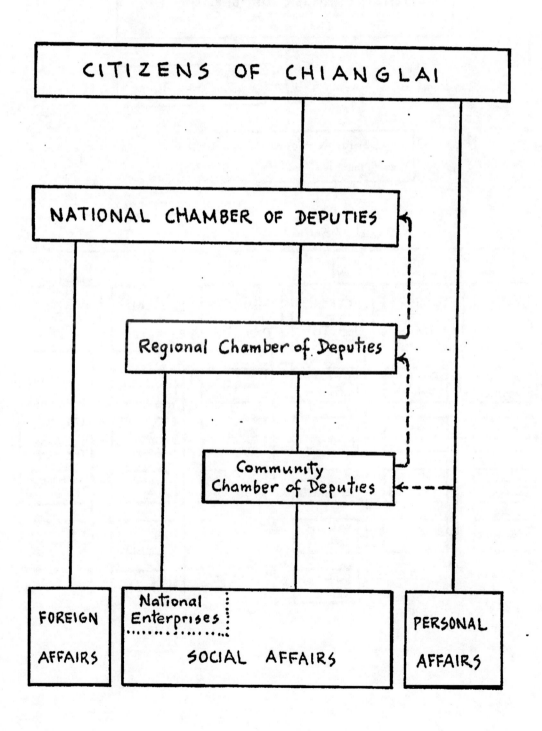

NATIONAL CHAMBER OF DEPUTIES

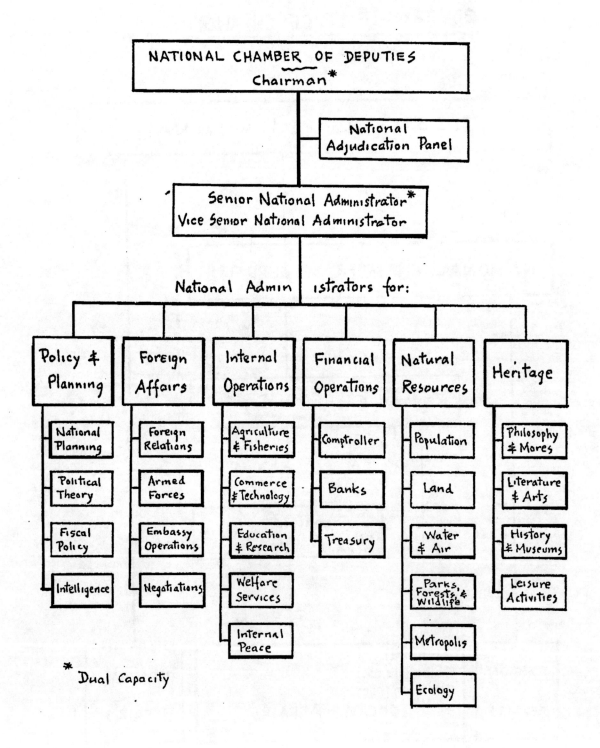

NATIONAL CHAMBER OF DEPUTIES
Chairman*

National Adjudication Panel

Senior National Administrator*
Vice Senior National Administrator

National Administrators for:

Policy & Planning	Foreign Affairs	Internal Operations	Financial Operations	Natural Resources	Heritage
National Planning	Foreign Relations	Agriculture & Fisheries	Comptroller	Population	Philosophy & Mores
Political Theory	Armed Forces	Commerce & Technology	Banks	Land	Literature & Arts
Fiscal Policy	Embassy Operations	Education & Research	Treasury	Water & Air	History & Museums
Intelligence	Negotiations	Welfare Services		Parks, Forests, & Wildlife	Leisure Activities
		Internal Peace		Metropolis	
				Ecology	

* Dual Capacity

REGIONAL CHAMBER OF DEPUTIES

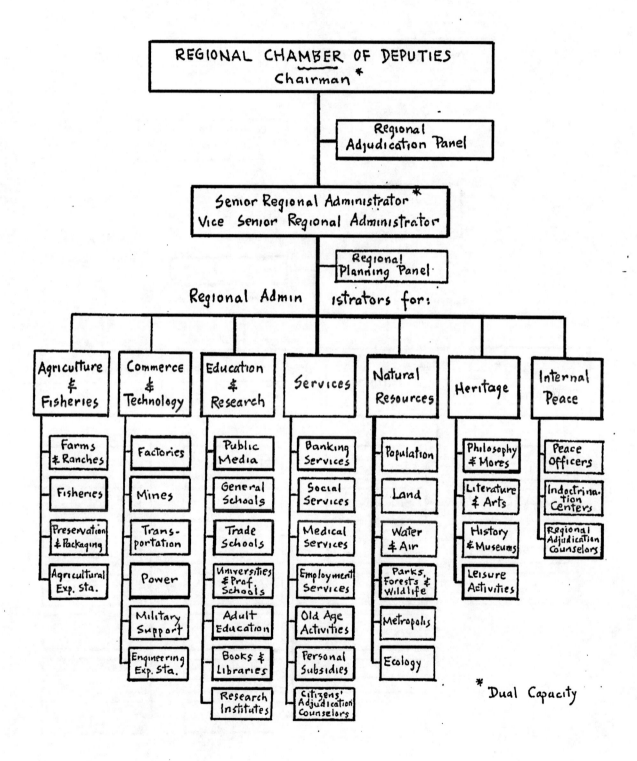

REGIONAL CHAMBER OF DEPUTIES
Chairman *

Regional Adjudication Panel

Senior Regional Administrator *
Vice Senior Regional Administrator

Regional Planning Panel

Regional Administrators for:

Agriculture & Fisheries	Commerce & Technology	Education & Research	Services	Natural Resources	Heritage	Internal Peace
Farms & Ranches	Factories	Public Media	Banking Services	Population	Philosophy & Mores	Peace Officers
Fisheries	Mines	General Schools	Social Services	Land	Literature & Arts	Indoctrination Centers
Preservation & Packaging	Transportation	Trade Schools	Medical Services	Water & Air	History & Museums	Regional Adjudication Counselors
Agricultural Exp. Sta.	Power	Universities & Prof. Schools	Employment Services	Parks, Forests & Wildlife	Leisure Activities	
	Military Support	Adult Education	Old Age Activities	Metropolis		
	Engineering Exp. Sta.	Books & Libraries	Personal Subsidies	Ecology		
		Research Institutes	Citizens' Adjudication Counselors			

* Dual Capacity

COMMUNITY CHAMBER OF DEPUTIES

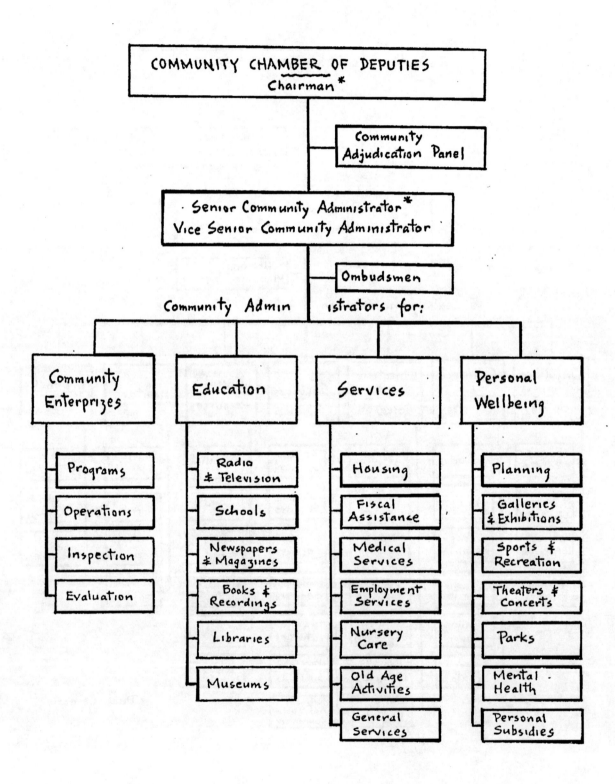

COMMUNITY CHAMBER OF DEPUTIES
Chairman *

Community Adjudication Panel

Senior Community Administrator *
Vice Senior Community Administrator

Ombudsmen

Community Administrators for:

Community Enterprizes	Education	Services	Personal Wellbeing
Programs	Radio & Television	Housing	Planning
Operations	Schools	Fiscal Assistance	Galleries & Exhibitions
Inspection	Newspapers & Magazines	Medical Services	Sports & Recreation
Evaluation	Books & Recordings	Employment Services	Theaters & Concerts
	Libraries	Nursery Care	Parks
	Museums	Old Age Activities	Mental Health
		General Services	Personal Subsidies

IV. Letter on Graciousness

My dear Honorable Senior Teacher:

Again I wish to express my deepest appreciation for your warm hospitality and instructive patience with which you explained your academic program in the Living Series, with the courses in Personal Well-Being, Social Well-Being, and Supporting Technics during my visit to Saikung University. The more I think about what you said, the more I am impressed with the significant conceptual advance you are making in bringing intelligence back into the human heart. This is the most hopeful sign on the educational horizon that I have seen for a long time and I earnestly pray that you will succeed not only in imparting this vector to learning in Chianglai, but also in diffusing it beyond her boundaries to such far-away places as America. To me this would be the greatest boon that can be bestowed upon my American brethren today.

You may be surprised at this turnabout in attitude from my skeptic questioning. I must have been rather obtuse in my unbecoming cocksuredness of "the most advanced country in the world." For such unbecoming conduct I must apologize most sincerely. My eyes have since been opened by my endeavor to fulfill the offer I had made to you.

You may recall that when I asked you for the capstone quality being conveyed to the students enrolled in the Living Series, you replied that it might be called—more as a reminder than a descriptor—graciousness. You then inquired as to our own views in America regarding graciousness. With rash confidence, I referred to the vast resources of our Library of Congress and volunteered to go over its card catalogue and send you a selected list of twenty books on the subject, as well as pertinent excerpts from my own files. I am afraid that, for the reasons outlined below, I will not be able to make good on the high expectations that I must have left with you.

Out of the millions of index cards at the Library of Congress, not a single entry was filed under the heading of graciousness. None of my own abstracts turned out to be of such direct and enlightening relevance as to merit calling them to your attention. The same disappointment was encountered with the *Book Review Digest*, the *Reader's Guide to Periodical Literature*, the *Great Books*, and the *Concordance* of the Holy Bible. I then perused the indices of shelves upon shelves of books on philosophy, psychology, sociology, personnel administration, management, English translations of Oriental writings, and so on. Still only incidental mention of graciousness.

Why is it so? I kept asking myself. Why is there such a neglect of what we immediately recognize, whenever we meet it in the flesh, as just about the most pleasing of human manifestations? Our own experience has repeatedly reminded us that a sense of penetrating satisfaction cannot be gained merely by being courageous in the discharge of our duties, assisting our fellow men in need, or forgiving them of their transgressions. To be courageous without graciousness can be brutalizing; to be of assistance without graciousness can be demeaning; to be forgiving without graciousness can be insulting. Even the traditional Western philosophical values of beauty, goodness, and truth can be constrained if not graced with graciousness.

A practical explanation that came to mind was that graciousness is not necessary for success in a highly competitive society such as ours. It may even constitute a self-imposed handicap. And since most of us here are driving ourselves beyond our native capacities, we feel disinclined to burden ourselves with this generosity of spirit. The tenor of our times discourages the requisite conditions of psychological affluence of time, empathy, and genuineness. They go contrary to our gospel of competition, with its rough-shodding urge to win in the arenas of power.

While this explanation may hold for men of affairs, it would not be as convincing in accounting for the inattention on the part of our scholars. In their case, it may be that they find it analytically more at home dealing with explicit elements rather than nebulous interpenetrations. As I reflect upon your discussion, I now understand your emphasis upon the pervasive nature of graciousness—how it reveals much more than the total experience of the individual, how it is actually the dénouement of the reciprocal kinship between two persons, how somehow the local universe, persons and all, it seems, dissolve in the fitness of the pleasing moment. With our strong attachment to the idea of property, that is, some trait or some thing must be ascribed to or belong to some body or some entity, it would be difficult for us to accept a gracious dénouement as belonging to neither subject, object, nor both—but to the *de-novo* totality.

But to me, the most surprising is the absence of a direct admonition either by Jesus Christ, Mohammed, or Buddha for men to be gracious—at least as recorded in the currently generally available English translations of their teachings. I can only ascribe this either to inadequate translations or to the worldly wisdom of these great men. They might have decided to pay first attention to alleviating the gross evils of hate, lust, vanity, and the like before embarking upon the finishing touches of graciousness. To be truthful, however, these conjectures are merely grasping at straws. Perhaps the essence is beyond words—as you yourself had implied. In the dumbfoundness of my failures, your point is finally sinking in.

Instead of continuing to look for expositions that can complete the sentence beginning with: "Graciousness is . . .," I tried your indirect approach. I went through various articles and books at random, mulling over those passages which might give some hint on one or more of the features, which may be part and parcel of the state of graciousness. In the process I began to see the light. It is still very dim, but your thoughts are now flickering in what was once a total darkness to me. Please permit me, as a student who is experiencing the delight of a new inspiration, to report to you on what I have found so far. I would be deeply indebted to you to set me straight, should I again be wandering off on the wrong path.

Above all, graciousness entails an artistic transmission of feeling from one person to another. This evocation cannot be hurried. A certain time is required to complete the gracious deed, within which a pleasing syncopation of expectation and reinforcement is built up and realized. It would be wrong to describe it as a quality or a capacity. It is more of a relational phenomenon.

It seems to me that one might not acquire a true perspective on graciousness if he overemphasizes the traditional starting point of many Western philosophical schools, namely the egocentric "What is the self?" Perhaps he should first focus his interest on the ultimate outcome of a human the situation and the manifestations of its pleasing harmony. Following this, he should then consider the proper execution of the act in accordance with pertinent means. Only after that should he seek clarification of the nature of the self and other contributory variables, which may or may not be of consequence in the attainment of the particular result desired. I see that I am running into the pitfall of analyzing consecutively instead of accepting the agglomerate of the instant. I am only seeking to suggest by this that when the self is the dominating consideration, graciousness is invariably precluded.

Graciousness arises then only in interactions between two persons. For this reason, one should consider and treat an individual as much as the situation permits as a human person, rather than a member of a category, class, or institution. In order to insure a favorable liaison on first encounter, one should make an extra effort to find out something about the other person beforehand. He should understand the behavior that is natural to him and adjust one's own moves accordingly. At the same time, the proper degree of cognition of one's own limitation should exist. This is ancient wisdom. The Egyptian vizier, Ptah-hotep, had so instructed his son over five thousand years ago and advised him to "discourse with the ignorant man as with the sage." One should not attempt to override the misgivings of others but let them dissolve through gentle and assuring behavior. This is particularly difficult when the reactions border on deeply ingrained emotions. Frequently it is nearly impossible to separate responses that are instinctive and therefore refractive to change from those that are acquired and therefore more amenable.

We are all familiar with the usual admonitions about being generous with compliments, about communicating with warm overtones, about embodying to one's words in concrete actions entailing some personal sacrifice if needs be, and the like. There are many occasions, however, in which the official requirements of one's position demand a tenacity and a stringency, which go beyond one's personal preferences. Even under such conditions one can be relatively gracious. In this case, he is not overbearing or officious. When he issues an order to a subordinate, he accompanies it with a clear indication of sympathy for the latter's feelings on the matter. When he is compelled to say "no" to men of goodwill, he does so without injuring their sensitivities or repudiating their well-meaning intentions. When he is engaged in a crisis, he conveys the sense of calm helpfulness through active participation. When he comes to the aid of others, he is quick to sense the core dilemma and resolves it directly and naturally. When he pursues his own ways, he does not embrace others who prefer to do otherwise.

One should not confound the gracious act with the polished words and graceful manners of the variety perfected by nineteenth-century courtiers and tutors of elegance. Rather it is more a matter of just the right thing to do under the circumstances. One might even draw an extreme illustration and say that the extra loud screaming for mercy on the part of an Eskimo woman being beaten by her husband may be regarded as gracious on her part if such ceremonial exaggeration regains the respect of her husband in the eyes of the community. The intensity of the action, of course, is not the determining factor. Like sonority in music, it may be loud or it may be an understatement. At times, there may be a touch of humor; at others, simply a kind of unconcern; at still others, a forgetfulness.

The self of the gracious man thus extends beyond the narrow self-centered confines to become part of the very event itself. All obligations are dissolved and all intentions reconciled in the atmosphere of mutuality. The giver does not feel a loss; the receiver does not feel an indebtedness. The entire affair is as natural as the blending of the sweet melody of the water-ouzel with the rumbling chord of the waterfall in the beautiful Sierras.

This is what you have led me to feel about graciousness. I am beginning to grasp what you might have meant when you said that the superior man is moved by contentment within and graciousness without.

With the greatest of respect and the best of wishes,

Your grateful pupil,

G.H.

Printed in the United States
2215